Philadelphia Story
A Lance Carter Detective Novel

Bruce A. Sarte

ISBN: 978-0-98395985-3-4

Credits
Editor: Jenn Waterman
Cover: Bruce A. Sarte

Bucks County Publishing
202 North 7th Street
Bally, PA 19503
http://www.buckscountypublishing.com

Dedication

This work is dedicated to my wonderful wife who is always supportive and helpful in my writing. Some people might call it enabling – but I call it love.

This work is also dedicated to the fantastic writers who have given me hours and hours of enjoyment and inspiration.

Acknowledgements

I'd like to thank Sean Sweeney for his thoughts and time when I'd bounce ideas and simple grammar off him. Having someone who writes and is straightforward as a sounding board proves to be infinitely valuable.

Special thanks goes out to my editor, Jenn Waterman for her stellar work under a tight deadline. And a final thank you to Natalie Springfield for reading the first draft and giving her input.

And a final thank you to Chris Aleckho, who several years ago called me and said, "Dude, I've got the perfect character for you. Linc Diesel!" The rest is now history!

Prologue

The wind whipped around my head like a cyclone on steroids. Rain pounding down with such ferocity it stung like tiny needles each time it struck my skin. Every few minutes I could feel it pool on my forehead just above my eyebrows before it spilled over into my eyes. Every drop of water made the cut on the side of my face burn like someone was rubbing salt into it.

Under normal circumstances, for most people, this would merely be an annoyance that would cause them to, perhaps, reach over and grab a towel. Not me. Not tonight. On this pitch black, stormy night, I was pushing the 427 in my cherry red 1969 Camaro Convertible hard. I had my baby hitting seventy-five miles per hour catapulting down Columbus Boulevard… with the top down.

I'm sure this immediately raises several questions in your mind. Where am I going? Why am I going there so fast? And why on God's green earth is my top down in the pouring rain? All those are great questions and I have answers to all of them. What I was lacking was the time to care about the answers. Unfortunately, this weather coupled with the difficulty I was having with the convertible top and other factors created a real need for a shot of liquid resolve. I reached over without looking and grabbed the bottle of Gentlemen Jack from the passenger seat. I deftly unscrewed the cap with one hand and pushed the cold glass to my lips. The amber liquid shot into my mouth like quicksilver and burned down the back of my throat like molten lava. Out of the corner or my eye I saw the light traffic light flip from yellow to red as I shot past the waterfront museum. Yeah, I saw it... I just don't care. I've got to get to the pier... I've got to get to the girl. I clumsily thumbed the top back on the bottle and tossed it into the seat just before I spun the wheel hard to the left. The back end of the car got a little loose but I feathered the clutch and hit the gas just in time for the rear to regain traction on the wet pavement. The engine roared as it passed the torque on through the driveshaft and gave the wheels the power they needed to catapult me into the parking lot of Pier 51.

The big ugly yellow warehouse sat there before me, mocking my approach. I saw it but couldn't focus... all I could think of were the words she said to me. The tone of her voice begging me to go save her little girl haunted my very being...

"Lance, please..." She sniffled her pain back inside herself. "Please save Jenny. I've got no one else to turn to." I felt her suffering through the phone in her throaty, dry voice.

"Lin, tell me what's going on. I can help you!" I urged her.

"Lance, there's nothing you can do for me – they are coming to get me!" I cut her off.

"Lindsey, tell me where you are, you have to tell me. I can help, I've got people – you know I've got people!"

"Lance, get to Pier 51 – go now! Hurry! They're coming here! They've already got Jenny! They're going to kill her!"

"Who? Who is it, Lindsey?" I yelled.

"It's... They are..." There was loud crash on the other side of the phone and Lindsey screamed.

"Lindsey!" I called out.

"Lance, please...." The sound of the gunshots echoing through the phone hit me right in the gut.

"Lindsey!" I screamed again and felt a cold numbness seep through me. *"Lindsey..."*

That was almost an hour ago. I had no idea what happened to Lindsey but I could only assume the worst. Deep down I knew that she wasn't all right. That nothing was right. I rubbed at my eyes and took another deep drag from the bottle. I came up around a corner and could see lights on top of each corner of the vomit yellow structure that had to be fifty years old as my Camaro tore into the parking lot. I slammed on the brakes and the car skidded to a stop square in front of the three-story dinosaur. The car was still jerking to a stop when I heaved the door open, jumped out and ran around to the north side of the building.

"Jenny?!" I called out.

I waited a moment but only heard the sound of the rain smacking the pavement and the river splashing up against the pilings of the pier. My gaze went from building to pier to the Benjamin Franklin Bridge off in the distance. The bridge was lit up like it was the fourth of July, only it wasn't. I directed my gaze at the boarded up skeleton of the *Moshulu* still moored at Pier 51. She'd once been a fine sailing ship and then a four star restaurant. Now she sat, crippled by fire, waiting for someone to save her... or the scrap heap.

"Jennifer!" I yelled with a sense of urgency in my voice. Again I listened and heard the dancing of the rain and the lapping of the waves. But then what was that sound? There was a rustling on deck of the abandoned ship.

I ran to the edge of the dock and looked from the bow to the stern of the three hundred and ninety six foot shop.

"Jenny! Is that you? It's me, Uncle Lancelot! Is that you?" I cupped my hands to my mouth to amplify my voice. I needed to make myself louder.

Then there was a muffled scream and then there were footfalls on deck. I pulled my Walther PPK, Betsy, from its holster and ran to where the gangway sat pitching back and forth to the rhythm of the river. I shook the padlocked gate fiercely trying to find a way around it.

"Jenny! I'm coming!" I could still hear the sounds of whoever it was moving towards the stern of the ship that faced Camden, New Jersey. I point my Walther at the lock and fired, shredding the lock into several pieces. I kicked the gate hard and it flew open, clanging into the metal posts of the gangway. With a quickness and agility I hadn't displayed in years, I bounded up the platform in four quick steps. I made a beeline for where I thought the noise was coming from.

I stopped and looked all around me. The rain was still coming down and the wind blowing in from the river made it very difficult to see. Then I saw her. The sight of little Jenny standing on the platform of the deck only inches from the railing sent a chill down my spine.

"Jenny..." I started but was cut off.

"If you take one more step, I'll off the girl..." The man with the gun pointed at Jenny's temple paused and then added with a sarcastic tone, "*Uncle Lancelot.*" He punctuated it with a maniacal laugh. I looked into Jenny's face and saw pure, unadulterated fear. She was frozen, not able to make a sound or move a muscle.

"Jenny, don't move. Everything is going to be OK," I tried to reassure her while slowly aiming my pistol toward the bad guy.

"You think so, Uncle *Lancelot*?" He nudged at her head with the muzzle of his gun. "What makes you so sure of that?" Jenny stumbled to the side as he poked at her. Her hair was matted to her head by the rain and a small, golden key dangled from a necklace around her neck.

I looked him straight in the eye and said, "This..." and pulled the trigger twice, placing two clean shots in his forehead. He had just enough time to register a look of shock on his face before he dropped his gun to the deck. The loud bang from his gun as it struck the deck was punctuated by a fire in my upper right thigh. I felt my leg go numb as I watched the bad guy free fall over the railing and into the river with a soft splash.

"Jenny!" I exclaimed with relief. I limped to her and took her in my arms in what seemed to be a feeble attempt to keep her safe from harm. On some nights it would have been enough. At this moment, not so much — but right here and right now, it was the best I could do.

"Uncle Lancelot, is it over?" Her small voice came to me through the rain. No one else called me by my proper name.

"Yes, honey... it's over," I replied, looking across the Delaware River to the Jersey side. Admiring how the lights from the bridge made the slums of Camden look like the Disneyland of murder and mayhem. But tonight it was the Philadelphia side that was filling my murder and mayhem quota with absolutely no help from Camden.

"She's dead..." Jenny said matter-of-factly. How did a ten year old simply work to the acceptance of the loss of her mother so quickly?

"Yes," was all I could say and I hugged her just a little tighter.

Chapter One

Ten Years Later

I could sit and stare out the window of my office all day long and the view never changes. My office has a fantastic view of the building right next door. The window was only about five feet away from mine. If I opened my window, I could touch the glass of the building next to mine. Yes, it is a glamorous life but someone has to live it, right?

Sitting in my chair with my feet up on the windowsill, if I angled myself just right I could clearly see Independence Hall and even a little of the mall. It was a great building. I could sit here and wax on about what great architects our founding fathers were and what brilliant lines the building had. But really I just like to sit and look at the place where the Constitution and Declaration of Independence were both born. Of course, anyone can see this very same building on the back of a hundred dollar bill... but seeing as that's not something I see very often, I look out the window. The sun's glare off the face of the clock was blinding me just a bit when my cell phone began to buzz on the top of my beaten wooden desk. The desk may be old and beaten, but it's solid and I love it. I grabbed the phone to keep it from vibrating off and smashing onto the floor in a million pieces. A quick glance at the screen revealed *Unknown* was calling.

"Carter Investigations, you lost it we'll find it. Lance here." My witty response to the violent ringing of my phone hung there for a minute. I could hear someone breathing on the other end of the phone so I tried again. "Hello, Lance Carter, can I help youuuu?"

"Um, no…" a soft, sweet sounding young female voice responded. "I think… I mean, I must have the wrong number." And just like that, she hung up. I shrugged my shoulders, dropped the phone back on my ink blotter and returned to staring at the two hundred and sixty year old birthplace of American freedom.

No sooner had my feet achieved their destination than my door swung open suddenly. Without even turning around I could feel the whirlwind that was my neighbor from across the hall bearing down on me.

"Carter!" Sally Ann Franklin started in on me. "Where have you been? I've been looking and watching and waiting for you but every time – No Carter!" My chair squealed in pain as I swung around to face Sally Ann.

"Good afternoon to you, too, Miss Sally," I said, trying not to make it obvious that the cleavage of her pert breasts had my full attention. She always wore her blouses unbuttoned down right far enough that you could see just the top of her bra on each side. Today the bra was black. I'm a big fan of the black bra under the white shirt.

"Carter, where have you been?" She propped her arms up on her hips, further accentuating her breasts. I wonder if she did that on purpose or if I was just a pig?

"Why? Someone looking for me?" I responded as aloof as possible while forcing my eyes to meet her cerulean blue spheres. It was difficult to do. Sally Ann Franklin stood about five foot two inches tall and had the body of a gymnast. She usually wore heels that added a couple of inches to her height and today she definitely had a nice pair on. I couldn't see them, but the way she held her hands on her hips told me they were nice. Her dark hair was pinned up in a loose bun that added a touch of professionalism to her young face. When she started shaking her black-rimmed glasses at me I knew she wasn't really happy with me.

"I," she emphasized this, "am looking for you! I never know where you are; you disappear for days... no, weeks at a time. Why don't you come into your office every day?" She put the glasses on her round, pretty face. The glasses were perfect for her. She had such a great fashion sense. I spread my hands out in a appeasing gesture.

"You *do* know what I do for a living, right?" That came out a lot more sarcastic than I'd intended. Sally Ann's stern gaze floundered for just a moment so I continued. "I'm a private investigator. I get cases... I go out on them and sometimes that means I am away. I didn't know I had to check in with you, den-mother."

Sally harrumphed at me, spun on her heel and stalked toward the door with a loud clack-clack-clack. She paused for a moment with the door open in her perfectly painted fingernails.

"I just..." Her voice was softer now. "I worry." She began through the door but I called out to her.

"Sally – wait!" She stopped and turned around quickly coming back into the office. Sally ran the Franklin Public Relations Company that had a small office down the hall from Carter Investigations. I'd only known her for about a year since she opened up shop but she was young and had a lot of drive to make her business successful. The problem was she was young and being young, she was very insecure. She'd made a habit of walking down the hall every morning and every afternoon since she opened her office. I'd hear her high heels clacking down the hall and see her form through the frosted glass of my door slow down just a little before continuing down the hall. She was checking to make sure I was here.

"Here," I grabbed a pen and scribbled down my cell phone number for her, "take this. If I'm not here and you want to know what is going on or where I am just give me a call."

"Thank you, Lance," she said quietly. "I appreciate it, I won't worry quite as much about *you* now," she added quickly with a small smile that made her face just a little bit prettier. Before I could say anything else, Sally Ann Franklin had slipped out of my office. The sound of the door clicking softly accented her heels clacking down the hall.

So just as I had before, I threw my feet up and stared out the window. I could see the people milling about. People walking across the street to the Constitution Center or maybe even to Benjamin Franklin's house. Some people standing in line on the corner, probably waiting for a horse drawn carriage ride to see all the historic sites. There were so many of them in Philadelphia. Just right here in a six block radius you could spend all day and still not see it all. Then I saw her walking from Independence Hall to the corner. Today her dark hair was in a pony-tail and bobbed slightly while she walked. I wasn't close enough to see her face but I knew what she looked like. I know how her misty blue eyes contrasted with her alabaster skin and how her hair made those eyes just pop out at you. I looked at the clock and sure as the sun it was 10:45. It might seem like I know this woman or maybe I'm a stalker but neither is true. She just reminds me of someone... someone who is... was very special to me.

"Carolyn..." I muttered softly and returned my gaze out the window. I threw my feet back up on the window sill and saw her face dancing across the window pane. Her beautiful blonde hair flowing over her shoulders and her smile that was so bright it seemed iridescent. She was one of those things in my life that seemed so long ago and so far away that at times I'd wake up and thought I heard her bare feet tapping down the hallway. Or I'd walk into the living room and smell her perfume. It was a lavender scent. She loved lavender and now, so do I. I shook my head and rubbed my face with both palms, feeling the unshaven stubble of my beard underneath them. Back to reality, as sad and lonely as that was at times. I was about to resume people watching with everything I had when there was a knock on my office door. Before I could respond to the knock, in walked an eyeful of the feminine form. I am pretty sure my mouth was open just a tad when my eyes went from her expensive burgundy pumps up her fishnet stocking covered legs and then I got stuck for just a moment on her knee length skirt that matched those pumps perfectly. She coughed, which drew my gaze up to her perfectly made up face.

"Do you mind?" she spat at me.

Not missing a beat, I replied, "Not at all. I'm quite enjoying it and it is my office after all." I looked back down to her feet. "Nice kicks, those Choos shoes?"

"Choos?" she replied with so much disdain in her voice you'd think someone in the room had just cut one. "These are Louboutin!" she announced emphatically and turned her ankle just enough to reveal a red sole to the shoe. "Only whores wear Jimmy Choo."

"Oh," I replied in my best fake startled voice, "who knew? I mean, not too many women stroll in here with a hundred dollar pair of shoes."

The look on her face was pure disgust. "Hundred? I wouldn't be caught *dead* in a hundred dollar pair of shoes. Try five hundred, mister detective!"

"Excuse me." I put my hands up in defense. "I was a little caught up in those long legs you have there." Leaning forward and throwing my best Bob Barker smile at her. She crossed her arms over her white blouse bringing it taut against her now noticeably firm and large breasts. She was one well put together woman.

"Do you speak to all your clients this way?" she said, looking down her perfectly formed nose at me. Seemed a tad too perfect the more I looked at it. Almost had a Michael Jackson feel to it.

"Are you a client? You seem more like a prospective client at this point."

"My name is Janet Pence. This..." She gestured behind her to the empty door and sighed in an annoyed manner before shouting, "Linda!" After waiting a moment, someone who I assume is Linda appeared in the door.

"Hi Linda." I waved at her. "Come on in and have a seat." Linda came through the door in a yellow sundress that barely concealed her more than ample breasts and hung down to her ankles. She looked to be in her mid-twenties with bleached blonde hair and perfectly blue eyes. She stood in front of me, a little bit awkward, fumbling with a lovely gold heart necklace that would have otherwise sat nicely between the valley of her tanned breasts.

"Hi," Linda sheepishly offered as she moved towards

and then sunk slowly into one of the brown leather chairs perched in front of my desk. Janet Pence made her way to the other chair but I put my hand up to stop her.

"I didn't ask you to sit. You were saying?" Janet looked at me hard.

"This," she pointed at Linda, "is Linda. Linda has a problem that we've been told you can help her with." She reached up with her nails that were painted to match the skirt and shoes to push some of her black hair from her face. I looked from her to Linda.

"So, Linda. You've got an issue you think I can help you with? How did you hear about my services?" Linda had her head down so that all I could see was her lovely dyed blonde hair and her dangly gold hoop earrings.

"You *are* a private detective, aren't you? Cam said you were and that you were very good," Janet answered.

"Cam?"

"Yes, he said you were very good at finding people and Linda needs someone found."

"Linda?" I looked at her wondering who the hell Cam was. "How can I help you?" Linda looked up at me, then at Janet.

"Linda's husband has taken her baby and run off!" Janet announced with a great flourish of her hands. "You must find him and get her baby back!" I looked at Janet wondering if her name was really Linda. I was taken by how the muscles on her neck played into her shoulders. She looked like she had been an athlete not too long ago. A swimmer? No, a dancer I bet.

"I'm taking your word for it that your name is, indeed, Janet, but every time I talk to Linda, you speak. How is that, exactly?" Janet pursed her lips and her eyes threw daggers at me. Man, she was attractive when she was mad.

7

I turned to Linda and spoke to her again. "Now, Linda. Tell me about it."

"Well," Linda began, unsure of herself. "It's Lenny. He's gone and he took Sammy with him."

"Lenny is such a loser…" Janet threw out there, in case I was interested.

"He is not," Linda shot at her. "Lar… I mean, Lenny… he just gets confused sometimes is all."

I leaned forward and put my elbows on my desk. "Tell me about it. What happened?"

"Well," Linda began, gaining a little confidence now. "Lenny was supposed to be home on Friday at six." She stopped and looked up at the ceiling as if a script was written up there for her to read and then continued without looking back down, "but he didn't. Then it was Saturday and he didn't come home and then Sunday and well today is Monday and he's still not home." I nodded my head in my best understanding manner.

"And Sammy?"

"Oh, yea!" She exclaimed now looking back at me. Out of the corner of my eye I could see Janet's face bunch up as if she was in pain. "He was supposed to bring Sammy home Friday. He always brings Sammy home from school on Friday." She nodded her head emphatically. I looked from her to Janet.

"He's an ass," Janet offered.

"Can you stand up for me?" I asked Linda. She looked at me with a confused expression. I nodded my head and waved her to stand. Linda looked at Janet before slowly beginning to rise and as expected, Janet interjected by placing her hand on Linda's arm.

"Why does she need to stand up?" she shot at me.

"Listen, Janet. As much as I'd like to lick fresh maple

syrup off that flat stomach of yours, you need to shut up now unless you have something to offer besides snide remarks and negative attitude."

"Well, I never!" She shot up in front of my desk. "Cam said you'd be like this."

"Oh he did, did he? Tell me, how do you know *Cam* exactly?" The detective beginning to detect.

"I used to clerk down at Judge Snyder's office. I knew him from my time there." I nodded my head now making the connection. Cameron Simile was a not-so-hot assistant district attorney in Philadelphia. Not much with digging up facts and people, so he'd call me every so often for small things like finding a guy who knew a thing about a thing. He slipped my mind because I never heard him referred to as *Cam*. This guy was no *Cam*. "And," she unfortunately continued, "how dare you speak to me that way!"

"Listen lady, I'd love to not *speak* to you at all. I have more nefarious things in mind that include," I began to tick off each finger, "syrup, whipped cream and cherries. But right now, it seems this poor girl may or may not need my help." I pointed to Linda who looked more confused than ever. "Now, if you don't mind, sit that perfectly rounded ass down and shut that expertly sticked set of lips. Thank you." She sat. "Now, Linda?" I gestured for her to stand again.

"Stand up?" she questioned.

"Yes, dear. If you don't mind." Linda stood in front of me and I looked her up and down. In particular I took in her very thin and young looking midsection.

"Is this good?" she asked, twirling just a little making the dress dance.

"Yes, it is. Thank you." I sat back contemplating that

this was a body that never pushed a baby from inside it. I whisked softly. "You are in incredible shape, my dear." Linda smiled and blushed before sitting back down. "How old did you say Sammy was?"

"He is seven." Janet answered matter-of-factly. I looked at her blankly.

Still looking at Janet, I continued, "And where does Sammy go to school, Linda?"

"I don't think Linda should tell you any more." Janet stated. "We don't know anything about your qualifications." She looked around my office, staring hard at my Felix the Cat clock on the wall. It's the kind where the tail ticks away the seconds and the eyes move in the opposite direction. A gift from a client a while back. I love that clock.

"My qualifications? Isn't Cam's reference good enough? I mean, he did say I was good… right?"

"Yes, but…" she paused, still looking around my office, "you aren't exactly in Liberty Place." I nodded.

"Janet, he doesn't…" Linda tried to jump in, apparently feeling uncomfortable.

"No, it's OK, Linda. I am thirty-six years old and have been a licensed private detective for six years now. I am about six foot two inches tall and weigh in in the neighborhood of two-hundred pounds. I'm a Cancer and my birthday is in July. More importantly I am a private detective… I detect things… find things… help people. You need something or someone found, I'm all over it. Husband cheating? I can help. Husband hitting you, I'm there. I don't do custody stuff. I'll find your husband and boy, but then it's your problem. I won't remove a child unless there is imminent danger and under no circumstances will I intervene in any dispute that does not have danger written all over it. I am licensed in the Commonwealth of Pennsylvania to carry a concealed firearm and I do. Regularly. Betsy is a Walther PPK. I'm a pretty good shot, too, if I don't say so myself." And there was that Bob Barker smile again.

"Betsy?" Linda questioned with a small smile.

"Yup, that's my girl." And I pulled Betsy out of her holster and placed her on the desk for all to see.

"Mr. Carter!" Janet stood and quickly got behind the chair. Clearly because everyone knows that leather chairs are bullet proof.

"Linda," I reached inside my desk drawer and pulled out a hello legal pad, "do you have pictures?"

"Pictures?" Linda looked confused.

"Yes, pictures. Sammy? Lenny?"

"Here." Janet reached inside her purse and produced two formal pictures. One of a man in his late twenties and one of a young brown haired boy.

"These Lenny and Sammy?" Linda nodded. The whole dynamic between these two was mind boggling. But I was still enjoying staring at Janet's svelte form so it was all good.

"Here," I handed the pad to Linda, "why don't you write down the address of the school and your address for me. I'll need the names of Sammy's teachers and some contact information for you, too."

"Wait," the annoying woman spoke again, "we haven't hired you yet. Are we on the clock now?" Now she's concerned with money?

"No," I began slowly, "I don't charge by the hour. I charge a flat fee and consider this a…" I waved my hands in the air and sat back in my squeaky chair, "a free consultation."

Janet looked at me very hard for a moment before saying, through clenched teeth, "Fine. Write down the addresses and names, Linda." She turned and stalked out of my office. Linda looked at me, uncomfortably again before scrawling down the information and handing me the pad.

"She's not always like this. She's just scared. You know, for Sammy."

I nodded, "And I'm sure you are too?" That seemed to catch her off guard.

"Oh, of course," she said with a small laugh. We exchanged finalities and I promised I'd be in touch once I'd spoken to some people.

I didn't know what to make of those two. One thing my keen detective instincts told me was that either Linda was blessed by the gods with a body that never quit or she did not have a seven year old son.

Chapter Two

I was still reeling a bit from Janet and Linda's little visit as I dragged my eyes over the names and addresses Linda had scrawled in curvy, flowery handwriting. I had just opened the lid on my MacBook to look up the addresses when my phone buzzed again with the familiar Unknown on the caller ID. I stared at it as the vibration moved it slowly across my desk. I hated *Unknown*. *Unknown* really wasn't ever very friendly and *Unknown* never called with good news. *Unknown* and I had a complex relationship. With a heavy sigh I picked it up the phone from my desk and answered the call.

"Hello, Carter Investigations…. If he's cheating we'll give him a beating," I said matter-of-factly. It was met with silence.

"Hello? Lance Carter here. Can I help you there?" I could hear the soft breathing again. It was definitely female, just like before.

"Listen, miss, if you need help I can help you but not if you don't talk to me."

"I…" her soft voice began but then stalled. I sat up, sensing something wasn't right. I didn't know what it was but my spidey-senses were tingling.

"Miss? Are you in trouble? Do you need help?" I waited for a response but again there was nothing but the soft breathing. "If you need help tell me where you are. Hello?" Suddenly the breathing was gone and the phone was dead. I pulled it from my ear and stared at the screen that displayed the time and my wallpaper of Citizens Bank Park on a bright sunny day. On a whim I pushed the slider on the display over to unlock the phone and dialed an old friend.

"Lancey!" she screamed into the phone while smacking gum loud enough that I pulled the phone away from my ear. "What's goin', babe?"

"Rhonda, I need a favor." Rhonda worked at a cell phone provider and could look up all sort of information on cell phone numbers. She was one of my many old clients that I remained friendly with. Satisfaction is always job number one at Carter Investigations.

"Of course, ya do. What's it today? You getting those heavy breather calls again?" She laughed a little too loud.

"No, doll… not exactly. I just got two phone calls and I'm afraid this person might be in a bit of trouble."

"Isn't everyone who calls you in a bit of trouble?"

"Yea, I guess they are."

"So I guess you wanna know where they are? What's the number?" The gum chewing stopped presumably so she could hear me better. The gum chewing was very loud.

"That's part of the problem. The caller ID comes up *Unknown* and I don't know who it is. I was hoping…" She cut me off.

"You were hoping that Rhonda could work her magic and tell you who it is and where they are." I smiled. "Am I right?"

"You know you are, Rhonda, baby."

"On your cell? Was the caller on a cell or landline?" she asked in a rapid fire manner.

"Yes and don't know but I think they were on a cell. Hard to say, just a hunch." I tried to match her rapid fire.

"OK, stud-muffin. I'll call you back... you give me ten minutes and I'll give you the world..." She hung up with that reference to the local news radio station hanging in the air and a smile on my face. Instead of just sitting behind my lovely antique wooden desk, I decided that I needed to visit my favorite coffee shop... Old City Coffee. A few stairs and a couple of blocks of walking had me putting the shoe leather to the brick sidewalks and passing below the coffee cup shaped sign into the best smelling café this side of the Mississippi. I did a lot of my best detecting sitting at one of these little round tables staring out onto Church Street.

With a steaming cup of Balzac Blend, I sat at the little table to wait for the lovely and talented Rhonda to return my call. Rhonda and I met several years ago when she hired me on a case to follow her deadbeat husband around who was chasing skirts. I dug up enough dirt on the scumbag to bury him. I thought that was the end of it. Unfortunately for Rhonda it wasn't. When she confronted him he beat her so bad she had to be hospitalized for a week. That didn't sit too well with me, so I did Rhonda a solid to make it clear that what he did was unacceptable. Rhonda thinks the broken jaw and flattened nose was the payback. But she'll never know the full truth of what payback from Lance Carter truly means. A man never hits a woman. And a man who likes all his appendages attached and functioning never hits one of my lady friends. I protect my friends and I defend my lady friends.

I was swirling Balzac in my mouth when Rhonda's

call made my pants vibrate and dance with digital joy. Quickly I set my cup down and fished my iPhone out of my pocket.

"Rhonda-baby, whaddya got for me?" The gum smacking preceded her words.

"The call came from an AT&T cell. I was able to pull up the number and the cell tower info if you want it?"

"That would be great, no owner info?"

"The account is a business phone. It's listed under Sparkle Industries, whatever that is…" she trailed off into another gum smacking fit.

"You got an address for Sparkle Industries there, doll?"

"Oh, Lance.." she clucked in disapproval, "you know I do. Here, I'm e-mailing you the whole account and cell tower info right now." I could here the clickety-clack of the keyboard in the background. "And send! You should have it in your inbox momentarily!"

"Rhonda – you're the greatest! What would I…." She cut me off.

"Lance, oh please… you know what you would do without me so let's not go there, 'k?" She let it hang for a moment before continuing in a more sing-song tone. "How about you take me out, buy me a drink, a little romance and then we play the who can sweat the most game?"

I laughed out loud, "Come on now, Rhonda, you know me better than that!"

"Yea, yea." She sounded disappointed. "No business and pleasure… I gotta get back to work, mist' Carter… "

We hung up and started to consider the phone call. I was being called by someone, a young girl presumably, from a business cell phone. It was owned by Sparkle Industries. What is that a dry cleaner? I decided another phone call was in order.

"15th precinct, how can I help you?" the very bored voice intoned.

"Hey now," I started off with my very best Howard Stern impression, "Lieutenant Faster Pussycat, please?" An old Navy buddy of mine had entered the Philadelphia Police Department right after he got out of the service and done quite well for himself. His name was Foster Phishkit, but I called him Faster Pussycat. Back in the service he was one of the fastest human beings I'd ever seen.

"Oh, he's gonna love you..." The less than polite officer put me through. After a couple of rings, he picked up.

"Phishkit here."

"Pussycat!" I announced

"Oh, for Christ's sake, Carter. What the hell do you want?" He loves me.

"I'm just calling to say hey, can't an old buddy just call to say hey?" I sounded hurt.

"When it's you, Carter?" He paused and then simply spat, "No!"

"Aw, c'mon old buddy, now you've hurt a poor, unfortunate soul's feelings. How could you?" The hurt in my voice increased to cartoon levels.

"You wanna get to the point here? I got murders to solve and a date at Geno's later. Chop chop." The irritation in his voice was still there, I wasn't making any headway.

"You mean a date *with* Geno's later..." I joked. Based on his silence, he didn't seem to find it amusing. "OK, listen buddy."

"Stop calling me buddy... when were we ever buddies?"

"We aren't? When did that happen?" I sounded

genuinely confused.

"Come on Carter, cut to the chase."

"Can do; I want to find out everything I can on Sparkle Industries. Criminal happenings or anything like that. Can you help a brutha out, my man?" Ending with my best Jimmie Walker impression.

"You want *what?* Carter, now you know I can't do that. How many times have we been over this? Ten?" I thought about it and he was right. Nonetheless, I pushed more.

"Sure you can, buddy. Remember Laundrocycle? You found some dirt for me, saved my client thousands of dollars. Be a pal...pal?" I heard him breathing through the phone.

"Why should I? To save your client *thousands?* Screw that. I'm on the taxpayers' dime here, not your megamillionaire client's."

"My mega what?" I wish. "Look, Foster, buddy... it's this girl. She's in trouble and I'm the only one who can help her. She's got no one else." I was one hell of a liar when I needed to be. "Do it for the girl, Pussycat."

"And you'll leave me alone?"

"Pinky promise." I lied again, but I think deep down, he knew.

"Alright, alright... I won't be able to give you any private information, you understand? No addresses or phone numbers. You need to beat the street and get that yourself."

"Already on top of that, muchacho."

"Gimme half an hour, I'll call you back." He paused. "Don't call me."

"Can do!" And he hung up. Foster and I were close at one point in the Navy. We were both SEALs and went on many missions together that we not only cannot talk about, but would most definitely not *want* to talk about. There was a lot of blood spilled between the two of us and here we were now trying to keep the blood from spilling. In the SEALs we fought side by side, often covering for each other when it was tight. During one raid in Baghdad we had just put two bullets in one of Saddam's Elite Guard's generals and were on our way out of the palace when Foster's electronics all failed him. He was essentially blind in the darkness that surrounded us. No one knew because he couldn't communicate. He came around a corner and tripped over something in his way and went careening down a flight of stairs. When I got to him he was unconscious and bleeding from the head. I picked him up and carried him three miles to the check point where a chopper picked us up. After that we were like brothers. Until I did something so monumentally stupid even I can't believer how dumb I am. I sipped my coffee just as the opening riff to *Smoke on the Water* rang out on my iPhone.

"Carter Investigations — if she's messing around, we'll take her down."

"Cute," Pussycat said, "very cute, Carter."

"Hey man, that was fast. You cops get a bad rap, I'll tell ya."

"Well this one was pretty easy, I can't tell you *what* is going on but I can tell you that Sparkle Industries in on our hot sheet. We've got eyes on every property they own — and they own more than a few."

"Really?" Now my curiosity was heightened. "Tell me more about my eyes..." I joked.

"No can do. All I can say is that if your girl can get away, she should. Far, far away... that's not place for a woman to be, Carter. And I mean that." The tone in his voice was clear and my attitude shifted.

"Understood, FP. I owe you one... next cheesesteak is on me."

"Yea, right... next time we do drinks. Because we do that all the time." And he hung up. I put the phone down and took another drink of my cup of hot goodness and pondered what Phishkit told me. Then my phone vibrated, I had a message. I picked it up and checked my inbox. Sure enough, there was an e-mail with the information Rhonda promised. I love technology and I love that Rhonda! It was time to find out more about Sparkle Industries.

Chapter Three

Less than half an hour later my Camaro rumbled up to what looked like an abandoned warehouse just east of Broad Street in south Philly. Sitting in the slightly worn cream-colored leather of my car I saw no apparent movement around the building. I sat and stared through my sunglasses at the old and apparently abandoned building. I killed the engine and shot off a quick e-mail to Rhonda on my phone asking if she was sure about the address. Now it was time to get a good look around.

My feet crunched on the cracking and broken sidewalk as I made my way toward the side of the building. The more I looked around the more convinced I was that it was abandoned. It was brick, about forty feet high with mostly broken or cracked windows. I turned the corner of the building and dragged my black cowboy boots into the broken up parking lot. But I stopped short as the full view of the parking lot came into focus. There were four cars parked in this beat parking lot behind an apparently abandoned building.

"What do we have here…" I muttered to myself as I slid my hand inside my jacket feeling for that little bit of extra confidence that only Betsy can give me. I love that gun and Betsy showed me her love every time I ran my finger over her trigger. I approached the cars slowly. They were all parked next to one another. I looked from one license plate to another noticing that three of them were from Pennsylvania, but one, the one closest to the door of the building, was from Jersey. Glancing around to see if anyone was watching, I pulled out my cell phone and took pictures of each car, then its accompanying license plate. I didn't know why but I had a sense that something here wasn't right. This was a broken down building in a beat up neighborhood with four cars parked in the broken down parking lot. I don't think that it was necessarily that the one car was from Jersey that raised the red flag… perhaps it was that the Jersey car was a perfectly maintained black Rolls Royce. I started humming the *Which One's Not Like the Others* song from *Sesame Street*. I thumbed the text message app on my iPhone, sent the license plate from the Rolls to Lincoln. Ironic, no?

Lincoln Diesel was my partner in the detective game. Linc had a life away from investigations but when I needed someone, when I needed an assist — Linc was my man. When you were standing in a barn and dropped the needle in that haystack, you called Linc to find it. Besides that, Linc spent twenty years as a Navy SEAL. I honestly don't know too much more than that about his time in the SEALs but I knew two things about him that came from his time as a SEAL: one, he was tough as nails; and two, he knew how to blow things up and make things dead better than anyone I knew. With all that in mind, I hit send and rested assured that Linc would find the owner in no time. Walking the length of the Rolls, I looked the door over slowly, noticing that it looked brand new. Like someone had just replaced it. It was solid metal and painted an ugly teal green color. I decided to leave the door be for the time being and give the windows on the side of the building a try. My head rose slightly up above the ledge of one of the many broken window panes. The inside was disheveled with trash strewn all over the dirty floor. I could see a mattress in one of the corners surrounded by what looked like crushed beer cans and unidentifiable paraphernalia. It looked like a typical abandoned building... except for another door. Right in the middle of the back wall was a brand-new looking metal door painted the same ugly teal color as the outer door. The only difference was this one had a slide-style peep hole in it. I heard noises from inside the building and the door swung open with an explosion of raucous laughter. Two young Hispanic men sauntered out, slapping each other on the shoulder and laughing hysterically. Must have been some joke.

"Yo, you see that?" the one on the left with a tattoo of a crucifix sans Jesus on his shoulder choked out.

"Yea man, that shit was off da hook, yo!" agreed the one on the right who sported two entire sleeves of tattoos on both arms. They both had assorted piercings and wore red bandanas on their heads to complete the street lowlife look. They were about four steps from that inner door when two things happened. First, that door slammed shut — seemingly catching them off guard because they both jumped when it happened. Second — and more troubling to me personally — my phone started to ring. I can be in the middle of a packed Old City Coffee shop and not hear that phone but I'll be damned if that thing wasn't echoing throughout the neighborhood now. I quickly reached down and hit the silence button but it was too late. The *boys from the hood* heard it and were on guard.

"Yo, who dere?" Crucifix yelled out, while Sleeves pulled a gun from behind his back and started waving it

Philadelphia Story by Bruce A. Sarte

around like windmill. I had to make a quick decision. My car was on the other side of the building and the only way there was past the outer ugly teal door. So I popped out from my hiding space and began walking around the parking lot like I was lost. It took Crucifix and Sleeves about ten seconds to burst out the door and spot me.

"Hey, who the hell are you, man?" Crucifix yelled.

"Whatyoudoinhereman?" Sleeves managed to put together in one word while still brandishing his firearm… now directly at me. I put my hands up, showing my iPhone to them.

"Oh, hey — yea man, sorry, I'm lost!" Plastering the best dumb look I could muster with a 9mm pointed at me. "Can you guys tell me where the airport is?" The airport? I deserve to be shot.

"What?" Sleeves started in. "You can't find the airport, yo? This friggin' moron. I should shootcher ass right now, boss. I should put you down just for bein' stupid, yo!" Sleeves was getting all worked up, but Crucifix looked at me longer and very carefully.

"Follow this road, take 95 south. You can't miss it," Crucifix said while taking me in from head to toe. "People like you don't last long in this neighborhood, you dig?" I slowly put my iPhone back in my pocket. But Crucifix's gaze had locked on the spot on my side where Betsy was sitting. I was sure he couldn't see her, yet he was staring right there.

"Yea." I started walking toward the Camaro, which I could just see around the corner of the building. "I dig." I had just been given a warning. I thought it was best if I heeded that warning… at least for now.

The Camaro roared to life when I turned the key but I stopped to look back at the parking lot. Crucifix and

Sleeves were both standing in the middle of the lot staring at me. I was sure that Crucifix had made a note of my license plate. I threw the car into first gear and gunned the 427, tearing away from the abandoned building that represented all I knew about Sparkle Industries and the phantom phone calls from the anonymous girl.

I had a feeling that this might be something left well enough alone. But my gut was telling me there was so much more to this then phone calls, Hispanic gang-bangers and an old warehouse.

Chapter Four

I rumbled into the parking garage feeling like I was abandoning her. I didn't know who she was yet somehow I felt like I had a responsibility to find her… to make sure she wasn't hurt and that she was safe. The Camaro slid into its parking spot and the engine went quiet. I sat staring at the cement wall letting my eyes run over the sign that read *831*. That was my apartment number. *The Benjamin Franklin House* was an historic apartment building located at 8th and Chestnut just outside what would be considered the heart of Center City Philadelphia. It was historic enough that the parking garage for the building was actually across the street, not in the building itself. That meant I had to walk across Chestnut Street. All in all this was not what one would consider a difficult or tedious task. Chestnut was and had been closed to vehicle traffic for as long as I could remember and there was a Dunkin Donuts on one corner and an Au Bon Pain on the other. They were no Old City Coffee, but in a pinch they would do.

Stepping past the Au Bon Pain, a lovely brunette appeared from the doorway and flashed me a million dollar smile. Being the gentlemen that I was, I stopped and smiled back. I resumed my way across the street by stepping on the curb but kept a keen eye on the twenty-something's short denim skirt that showed more skin on her tanned legs then it covered. And that blue t-shirt that was sitting just askew off her shoulders with the faux ripped collar and no sleeves had my full attention while it bobbed gently revealing just a hunt of lower back flesh. It was about at the point that I was taking in her black high heels and biting my lip that I felt it come out of nowhere. The impact lifted me off my feet and threw me several feet. I'm not sure in what order my body hit the ground because I blacked out. When I opened my eyes it was blurry but I could make out a face above mine and it... no, she was saying something to me.

"Mister... hey mister, are you OK?" she was shouting but I didn't have it in me to respond quite yet. My vision cleared to see that it was my lovely little brunette nymph with the short skirt and killer heels. "Sir? Can you hear me?" She paused and looked around at a few people who were watching. She reached inside the pocket of her skirt and pulled out her cell phone. I was beginning to regain my faculties and grabbed her wrist.

"No, no, I'm fine..." I began but as soon as I tried to move, a bolt of pain shot through my head. "Oh dear lord, what the hell happened?" I muttered.

"Please," she said plaintively, "let me call 911 and get you some help. You need an ambulance." I began shaking my head no but the pain made me stop that quickly. "I'm a med student at Jefferson, listen to me." She looked around. "Does anyone have a jacket or sweater?" No one answered but I could imagine people were shaking their heads. It was the middle of June after all. I could see the moment of indecision on her face just before I watched her sit straight up and quickly pull the blue shirt over her head revealing her lacy blue strapless bra that held in her ample breasts. I'm quite certain that my eyes widened at the sight of her young firm torso but she didn't seem to notice. She was too busy bunching up her shirt and placing it under my head.

"I... I'm OK, really, just..." I put my hand up. "Someone please help me up?"

"No!" she practically yelled at me. "You could have a concussion. That bike messenger should be arrested." She looked away from me. "No idea how he didn't wipe out and kill himself. Asshole!"

"Someone?" I repeated a little louder as I began to push myself up. Some guy in a Metallica t-shirt came over to give me a hand and my lovely half naked med student grabbed my shoulder too.

"You really..." she began but I cut her off.

"Hey, I really appreciate what you're doing here..." I stopped putting my hand to my forehead as my vision blurred just a bit. "Especially with the whole nudity thing, big motivator... very nice, really. They..." I stopped and scrunched my eyes in momentary embarrassment. "it... you... I'm good, really, all set."

"Are you sure?" she asked with a level of concern that I didn't fully understand. Either she was as smitten with me as I was with her or she was going to be a fantastic doctor.

I smiled at her baby blue eyes and spread my arms out wide. "I'm as good as new, and as much as I hate to do this," I reached down and handed her the blue shirt, "you can put your shirt back on now." She took it from my hands tentatively. "If you still feel bad for me, you can do it slowly." I ended that with my most charming smile.

She cracked an open mouthed smile and looked down slightly embarrassed. "Real nice," she remarked as she tugged the shirt back over her head. It got caught for a second on her pony tail but just as quickly as it was caught, it bobbed back out. The skin show now over, the crowd began to disperse. I waved to them with my best princess wave and muttered, "Thank you, come again!" in my best Apu impression.

"You seriously need to get checked out, you might have a concussion. Do you live alone?" I was looking at her, trying to gauge the direction her question was going, and then she continued. "You really shouldn't be alone if you have a concussion." Not the direction I was really hoping for.

"Ah, well yes," I stumbled through the words, "just me and my Copper." Stumble stumble. "Copper, he's my pup... you know, dog... woof?" I wasn't sure if my inability to articulate was the blow to the head or the image of her topless and leaning over me that was indelibly burned into my mind. I nodded at her. "Thank you again for stopping, it was very kind of you." I turned and walked to the other side of the street only to catch my foot on the curb and fall face first on the sidewalk.

"Motherfucker!" I yelled as the blood poured from my nose.

"Stay still!" Her voice came from behind me and then she was there. "Roll over slowly, let me look."

"Dammit!" My hands were covering my nose but I could see her surveying my newly damaged schnoz. She touched the side of my face and then my nose; I instinctively slapped her hand away. "Shit that hurt!" Immediately I felt bad. "I'm sorry I didn't mean to be all sloppy..."

"Well come on, let me look, Sloppy." She smiled at me with that million-dollar smile and I dropped my hands. "Here, sit up." She helped me into a sitting position.

"Well, Doctor Skin, what's your diagnosis?" I prompted after a moment of her prodding.

"It's not broken just beaten and battered. Here," she stood and offered me a delicate hand with perfectly blue painted fingernails, "up with you."

I accepted the help and got to my feet. As soon as I did my balance betrayed me but Doctor Skin was right there to steady me.

"You live here?" She tilted her head toward the building and I nodded affirmatively. "Come on, big guy, let me at least help you home?" I agreed by walking into the lobby with her. We entered the two hundred year old lobby arm in arm as if we were a couple. With each step across the marble floor toward the elevators my head cleared a bit and was feeling better. I was pretty sure I wasn't going to let my little brunette almost-doctor know that though. I nodded to Sanjay, the security guard, and we walked past. He stopped what he was doing long enough to look us over with an approving smile and nod in our direction. We stopped at the elevator. She leaned away from me, no longer supporting my weight and pressed the up button.

"Love the nail color." I said, trying to break the ice a little on a more personal level. The sudden attention on her nails made her pull her hand back and look at them for a moment.

"Yea," she began thoughtfully, "I felt like it was a *blue* day... you know?" And suddenly in the moment that she cocked her head, she went from helpful-medical hottie to too-young-for-me hottie. The elevator arrived with a ding and a swoosh of the doors.

"Say, thanks for the help but I'm feeling much better. You don't have to come up. I'm fine."

"What, you mean you are going to leave me here in the lobby? What will your security guard buddy think if I don't come up for at least an hour?" She smiled at me wickedly and I couldn't say no as she stepped into the elevator with me. "Floor?"

We arrived at my apartment door and my head really was quite clear at this point. I pulled my card key out and opened the door to my two bedroom apartment. The door opened into a small hardwood floored dining area with the bedrooms to the left, the kitchen to the right and the beige carpeted living room straight through the dining area.

"Not bad," she started before I turned around to stop her in the doorway.

"Name?" I prompted her.

"What?" She was caught off guard.

"I got run down in the street and opened my eyes to see this stunning young woman taking care of me. Now she is about to enter my apartment because she was kind and insistent enough to make sure I was well enough to be on my own. I would like to know the name of my Florence Nightingale." She smiled and I thought I saw her cheeks flush just a little. "Or do you like Doctor Skin?"

She shook her head. "Not especially... but I've been called worse. Nathalie, the French spelling."

"The French spelling? What is that exactly? Spelling with attitude?" She laughed.

"No, with an H after the T. Don't ask me, it's my whacked out parents." She said as she rolled her eyes.

"Oh, I see... how exotic in a pointless kind of way." My turn to smile at her. "And I am Lance. Lance Carter." I offered her my hand.

"Pleasure to meet you," she shook it, "Lance."

"And this," the jingle of the collar signaled my Shetland sheepdog's entrance, "is Copper."

"Well, hello Copper," Nathalie reached down to offer a pat on the head in greeting. "Now, Mister Carter, you go lie on the couch and point me to your bathroom." She held up her hands to reveal blood on her palms that I had not noticed before. "Since you were so kind to bleed on me, might I trouble you for a sink for a rinse up?"

In spite of the imagery in my head of her *rinsing* up, I pointed down the hall and watched her nice behind wiggle down the hall to the bathroom with Copper in-tow. On my way to the couch the bar in the corner caught my eye. Since I saw it, I thought it appropriate to not ignore it. I poured myself a Jack on the rocks.

"Nathalie with an H," I yelled out, "can I get you a drink?" I could hear the water running in the bathroom.

"Yea, sure," she yelled back. "It's been a long day, any chance you have some Jack Daniels?" I smiled to myself but did not answer her. This was my kind of girl. When she came into the living room, I was sitting on my rustic brown leather couch with two drinks in hand.

"One for you and one for me." I handed her a glass with a smile and offered up a toast, "To my doctor savior."

She shook her head and took the glass. She sat down facing me with a leg tucked under her about a body width away. "Med student, not doctor," she aptly corrected me.

"OK, Med Student Nathalie with an H. Tell me, how old are you exactly?"

"Twenty four," she replied a little shyly. "But I'm in my last year of med school — doing rotations. I'm on my orthopedics rotation now at Hannahmen and that wraps up in two weeks, then I start a psych rotation back here at Jeff." Hannahmen was one of the hospitals on the other side of Center City along with Jefferson Hospital and Medical College.

"Ouch." My face crinkled and I took a big drink "Twenty four??" I said in disbelief.

Philadelphia Story by Bruce A. Sarte

"What?" she said, slightly offended. "How old are you? Thirty?" She sipped at her drink.

"I'm not sure how to feel about that but no, I'm thirty six"

"Oh." She took a bigger drink this time. "Well, it isn't like we're sleeping together or anything. Right?" she asked with a raised eye brow.

"No," I replied as professionally as possible, "at the moment, we are sitting on the couch having drinks. How is it that you are so young, yet almost Doctor Nathalie with an H?" She smiled.

"I was part of an accelerated program at Penn State. Two years of Penn State Pre-Med and four years of Jefferson Medical and voila, Doctor Nathalie Tomei."

"Tomei?" I asked, "As in Marisa?"

She blushed and looked down at her drink before taking a drink. "Yes, she is my aunt."

"Ha! I knew it!" I exclaimed, "I knew you looked like someone famous. That's who it is. Marisa Tomei." I stopped and immediately felt bad. "Oh hey, I'm sorry. You probably hear that all the time.

"No, it's OK. I usually don't tell anyone about it. I didn't even know my dad was her brother until two years ago. So enough about me, what does thirty-six year old Lance Carter do for a living to have such a nice apartment complete with carpet and a luxurious leather couch?"

"I'm a private detective... I detect things," I said in my best private detective voice.

"Really?" she said, smiling. "You detect things?" She finished her Jack Daniels.

"Yes, lost puppies, lost people, missing cats or cars. I'm your man. Lance Carter, Super-Detective. No H in that."

She stood up from the couch and placed the glass on the side table. "Well, Lance Carter Super-Detective, you look fine to me so I'm going to go." She reached over to the coffee table and grabbed the pen sitting on a copy of Guns and Ammo magazine. She ripped a page out and scribbled on it. "Here's my cell number. If you need…" she paused and looked at me, "anything. Call. OK?"

I stood to take her number and look her in the eyes. "I sure will."

"And if I need anything… detected?"

"You'd better call," I said firmly.

Chapter Five

After Nathalie left I was able to unwind on the couch with Copper and another glass of Jack Daniels. It wasn't until my phone began ringing did I remember that I missed a call while being accosted by the inner city version of Menudo.

Unknown. Great... my favorite caller.

"Hello?" I offered, hoping for a response but just like earlier in the day, nothing. It was actually starting to get on my nerves considering the kind of day I ended up having. "Look, I know that you are with or work for #1 Velvet Dragon Industries and I know where the warehouse is so I'd really..."

"You shouldn't have come to the warehouse today," she interrupted in a flat monotone.

"No? Why not? You..."

"Javier and Miguel will shoot you," she interrupted again in the same flat monotone. So that's what Sleeves' and Crucifix' names were. Wonder which was which.

"Your Hispanic friends don't scare me. I was just trying to make sure you weren't in trouble." I paused hoping for some input from my mystery caller. "Are you in trouble?"

"I... I..." she stammered, unsure of herself suddenly.

Philadelphia Story by Bruce A. Sarte

"I should have never called you, I just want to tell you not to worry and that it was a mistake for me to call you." Her speech pattern had increased almost to the level of panic. "Just stay away... they will hurt you and..." She stopped suddenly and let her words hang.

"And?" I prompted.

"Nothing," the flat tone had returned, "just stay away."

"Who is this? Why are you calling me?" No response. "Hello? Are you still there?" But the mystery girl was gone. Just like before, I didn't have anything tangible but I felt like something was wrong and I was responsible for this girl. And somehow, she felt a responsibility for... me?

I looked at my missed calls and saw it was Linc who had called earlier.

"Lance. Linc. Call me. You want to know who's car that is." He said it matter-of-factly, as if I *wanted* to know who's car that was. Not implying a question. So I did as instructed by my venerable partner of few words but many skills.

"Hey Linc!" I said in my best mobster impression. Linc loves it when I poke fun at his Italian heritage. "Wassa happening!" More ethnic humor.

"The car is registered to Soriano Mustafa." That Linc, always right to the point. But this little piece of information caught me off-guard.

"Say what now?" Soriano Mustafa was one of the biggest crime bosses this side of New York City and the word was that he even had ties up there.

"And do you want to guess who is listed at the owner of #1 Velvet Dragon Industries?" Linc added in his gravely baritone.

36

"Soriano Mustafa?" I wagered a guess.

"Bingo." His gritty voice stayed steady.

"You didn't happen to see what #1 Velvet Dragon Industries does exactly?" I took a shot.

"They are listed as an import and export enterprise. But I made some calls." Linc is nothing if not thorough. "You familiar with Savannah's?"

"Of course." Savannah's is a high-priced, elitist gentlemen's club. It was the kind of place that had a membership fee per year, not a cover charge. Only the wealthiest people were members. Only the youngest and most beautiful women danced at Savannah's. There were rumors that for the right price, anything could be had. "You know, I've *heard* of it."

"Number 1 Velvet Dragon Industries owns eighty percent. They also own a stake in the Maritime Museum and The Moshulu."

"So why does this make me want to find this girl even more, Linc?"

"What girl?"

"These calls I've been getting... I was just on the phone with her."

"Who is she?"

"That's the thing, I have no idea. But I think she's in trouble. She keeps calling. I think she needs help but won't ask for it."

"Hmph." Linc had a way with words.

"Yea, that's how I feel about it too."

"Need me on this?"

"Not now. Maybe later."

"OK." And Linc hung up. Linc talks too much.

I downed the rest of my Jack Daniels and decided that something had to be done. I had to find this girl, whether she liked it or not. Maybe that warehouse would have a bit more going on at night.

* * *

I dropped the top on the Camaro, jammed the pedal to the floor and sped out of the parking garage back towards South Philly and the #1 Velvet Dragon warehouse. After a twenty-minute drive I cut the lights and rolled up about a block away from the warehouse. There were over a dozen cars in the parking lot now. I raised an eyebrow as my vision went from Cadillac to Lincoln to Mercedes to Infiniti. It appeared as though #1 Velvet Dragon Industries did a swimming business in the evening hours that seemed to cater to people with a little bit of cash.

I sat for a couple of minutes watching the door when a set of headlights came around the corner. The car slowed almost to a stop before pulling into the parking lot and sliding into the space next to the Maserati. I was too far away to see their faces but I watched two exceedingly tall men get out of the dark colored BMW 7 series sedan and walk up to the ugly teal door. The men, who could have been on the Sixers, both paused at the door, looking a bit confused. Then the man on the left turned to the other to say something. The well-dressed man on the right didn't even acknowledge the slightly less-dressed man, he swung the door open and waltzed through the pinnacle of teal-ugliness.

"Don't they look familiar..." I lamented to myself. "Well, Lance, maybe it's time you had a closer look... when this place is open."

I fired up the engine and pulled the Camaro in right next to the BMW. I pulled on the tweed sport jacket I kept in the back seat for just such an occasion and ambled to the door of tealness. Just like Kareem and Magic before me, I paused at the door and looked around. I didn't pretend to say something to my imaginary friend... but he was there nonetheless. I reached down to turn the knob on the door only to discover it was locked. I jiggled it to make sure I wasn't just being a spaz, but it was locked. I was certain that the dude who looked like Mo Cheeks just opened the door with no problem. I stepped back to survey to door again, make sure I wasn't missing anything. That's when I noticed the small video camera attached to the building just above the door.

"Crap!" I exclaimed out loud just as I heard the door click. "No crap?" I reached out, turned the knob and the door popped open. Smiling, I swung the door open and entered the dingy warehouse. It looked very much as it did earlier in the day, just darker. I made note of the other teal door on the back wall that I'd noticed earlier. I could see light flashing underneath the door and club type music pumping from behind it. Was this just an elaborate guise to hide a nightclub? I shook my head, "No, come on, Lance. Sometimes a cigar is really a joint..." I felt for Betsy and found her where she belonged before I moved quickly to the inner teal door. I put my ear to the door and could make out the chorus of Madonna's *Like A Virgin* oozing from behind the door.

I grabbed the door knob and pulled open what appeared to be nothing less than the door to Pandora's Box. The music hit me in the face before the smoke enveloped me. I closed my eyes in an effort to shield them from the smoke and sudden change in ambient light. I could practically taste the menthol in the cigarettes and smell the liquor someone had spilled somewhere. It was nothing less than a full-on assault on my senses. The only thing that wasn't being bombarded was my sense of touch, until I felt something soft and warm brush up against me.

"Hey stud," Miss Soft-and-Warm whispered in my ear, "wanna to buy me a drink?" My eyes fluttered open, still battling the flashing lights and smoke, to see a short yet adorable young girl looking up at me with a smile more brilliant than the lights on the stage. I tried my best to return the smile but think I failed because her smile shrunk just a bit before she tried again. "What's wrong, big boy? Never seen a sexy young bunny before?" I hadn't taken full notice of her attire but she was right on. She was dressed in a red velour bunny suit that looked like it came right out of Heff's closet in 1975, complete with fur trim around all the naughty parts.

"I can tell you," I began in an awkward and stumbling manner, "I've never seen anything quite like you before." I bit my lip as I looked her over, just for effect of course.

She flashed that electric smile at me again and cocked her head over so sexily-slightly and laid out what had to be her closing line. "Well a pretty girl like me just can't drink alone, now can she?" And then she sealed the deal with a couple of bats of her foot-long eyelashes.

"No, no, we absolutely just couldn't have that, now could we?" She shook her head slowly, took my hand and led me towards the bar. She slid her compact, firm frame onto the soft, velvety bar seats and patted the one next to her as an invitation to join her — so I did. The bar was made of see-through glass and lined at the edge with a dark-stained oak for resting your arms on. It was very eye-catching. I looked over at the stage area and spied a perfectly gorgeous brunette wearing a very revealing black bikini with a matching pair of high heels. She strutted down the runway of the stage, spun on her heels almost in-time with the music and with one motion of her delicate fingers popped the back of her top off to reveal two of the most perfect breasts in creation. It was about the moment that I was certain that they weren't real that I realized this wasn't a night club — it was a strip club. I moved my eyes slowly to my new companion, keeping the smile plastered to my face and began wondering to myself if she was just some cute girl looking for a free drink or if she was a hooker.

"So," I began loud enough for her to hear but trying not to yell, "what's a pretty girl like you drinking this evening?" I looked up and down the bar but didn't see a bartender. "And where's the bartender?" She didn't answer me. She just cocked her head again but this time with a slightly confused look on her face.

"You're new here? Aren't you?"

I laughed. "Is it that obvious? I... I just got, you know..." I let it hang there hoping she might fill in the blanks. Thankfully for me, she picked up right where I left off.

"Yea, Mister M's people haven't been giving the new clients the details like they used to. You see those stairs over there?" She leaned in and pointed to the other side of the stage. "Let's you and me go on up there and have a talk, shall we?" She ended it with a smile but got up and walked toward the stairs without waiting for an acknowledgement from me. I stood up and began to follow her just as the dancer's bottoms fell to the floor and she twirled them off the edge of her toes. I stopped for just a second and looked at the girl. She appeared to be tall, in very good shape and put together like a Barbie doll. I shook my head as I decided that not only were her breasts not real but her facial features didn't look right. Almost as if she had been sculpted. I tried to catch up to my little bunny but was starting to get a nagging feeling that this was more than just a strip club and that girl wasn't just *stripping her way through college.*

When I got to the top of the stairs, Miss Bunny was waiting for me inside a room directly to the left with a velour curtain pulled back. I followed her into the room. The room was smallish, about ten by twelve with red plush couches along three walls and the curtain on the other. The carpet was a shag of a deeper red color.

"Very nice..." I commented as I took in the scene. Bunny closed the curtain and pushed a button on the wall. "What's the button?" She walked over to me and gave me a shove, depositing me firmly onto the couch. Without words she straddled me and began gyrating her hips slowly just above my lap without actually touching me.

"Now," she began in a deeper voice. It wasn't quite sensual but it was laced with sexuality. "When someone asks you for a drink here — you would respond with what you want. For example, a Long Island iced tea would get you tall and thin, while a Harvey Wallbanger would be something shorter and rounder... you follow?" I couldn't believe what I was hearing. What... where was I? But I nodded my head very absently. "If you aren't sure, just ask what the specials are and your concierge — that would be me tonight — will take care of the rest."

"Specials?" I asked in disbelief.

"Yes, I've already done that for you tonight. But be forewarned not all the concierges are as understanding as I am. If you don't know what you want, or understand how to ask for what you want, they won't help you like I've done. Please remember that when Mr. M asks."

"Mr. M?" Before Miss Bunny could answer there was

a soft tone that seemed to come from nowhere and everywhere at once. She slowly lifted her left leg off me and pulled her right one back. She lingered close to me for a second before backing away and exiting the room with a smile and a wink. No more than a minute later, a girl who couldn't have been a day over twenty years old slithered through the curtain. There was the sound of a door shutting behind her but I'm not sure where the door was. She stood with her body half hidden by the curtain and looked at me. She was frozen for a second and I thought I saw a look of recognition cross her face but it was gone as quickly as it was there. Slowly the rest of her emerged and I got a full look at her lean and taut body that was encumbered in black leather. Her form was covered in black leather accented with black lace with just enough skin showing to make you look and but not enough to make you want to look away. Her vanilla skin accented the outfit and looked more like it belonged on a Victorian couch not swinging from some metal pole in a place like this. Her lips were painted a deep ruby, her dark hair was pulled back tightly, making her green eyes pop in contrast to her light skin. She was stunningly beautiful. She stalked over, dropping to her knees right in front of me with a devilish grin on her face. She stared at me forever before she leaned forward and mouthed, "Be careful what you wish for when you dream." I could feel the dollar bills pushing to be first in line to jump out of my pocket.

"Hi..." I offered awkwardly, trying to prevent any clothing from being removed any time soon. She looked at me like I had spoken Greek and then penetrated me with her deep emerald eyes. In that moment I felt naked and knew it was a bad place to be. When she put her hand on my chest I spoke up.

Philadelphia Story by Bruce A. Sarte

"I'm L..." She put her finger to my mouth but continued to look at me oddly. "Look," I said, "I'm not here for this. You don't..." She bolted upright as if someone had given her an electric shock. She began backing away shaking her head back and forth. With her hair swaying she ran from the room. I heard the door, which wasn't there when I came in, open but didn't hear it close. I quickly stood and took two steps toward the curtain but was quickly curtailed by the presence of two large Asian men wearing black suits and black sunglasses.

"Hey guys..." I offered with a laugh and my hands raised showing no resistance. "I didn't touch her. I swear!" I pointed toward what I assumed to be the exit behind them. "I was just leaving, so if you'll just," I made a moving motion with my hands, "ya know, move aside?"

There was one guy on the left with a small scar above his right eye. He simply shook his head no. So I decided to try and walk between then. The guy on the right, who has a diamond earring, placed his big paw on my shoulder, which effectively stopped me in my tracks.

"Now, come on here, guys, no need for touching." I reached up and attempted to remove the heavy hand to no avail. I was about to explain to him how bad an idea touching me was when I heard a scream from outside the room followed by something falling to the floor. So I grabbed his thumb, twisted his wrist and enjoyed the sound of his forearm shattering. He yelled out something in a language that I didn't know and crumbled to the floor. His partner reached out to grab me, so I countered by grabbing his hand and striking upward with my palm, breaking his elbow. With my new Asian buddies on the floor, I pushed through the curtain to the hallway, glancing around for the source of the scream. I pulled Betsy from her holster and

44

began making my way down the hall filled with curtains on each side. I didn't hear anything coming from anywhere so I pushed a curtain aside to find a sliding door.

"Oh, so that's where the door comes from…" I pushed the button and slid the door aside. I found a fully nude, fully erect man behind a young and pleasantly round young woman. He was spreading something that appeared to be oil on her back and butt, seemingly enjoying every minute of it. I burst into the room and made them both jump up. Naked dude dropped the bottle of oil on the floor. While the oil gushed onto the floor he put his hands up and starting whining.

"I didn't… no, don't… I swear…" I looked from him to Betsy and then pointed it at him.

"Get. Out. Now." Before I could finish my directive he had his clothes in his hands and was pushing past me out the door. Scum.

"What the hell are you doing, motherfucker!?" The portly red-headed woman was coming at me now with her very large breasts bouncing happily in front of her. "You gonna pay me his tip? Fuck no, you ain't!" She punctuated her anger with a fist to my groin. I went down like a wet paper towel. In a ball and in intense pain, I had just enough sense to make sure I still had Betsy in my hand.

"Wade! Maurice! Someone!" She was yelling down the hall. She turned back and started kicking me in the back. "You asshole, that's my rent money you're stealing from me!"

"Stop!" I put a hand up. "I'm just… shit!"

"You're just talking food out of my mouth, you asshole!" She didn't stop kicking me but I was able to recover just enough to get out of the room before my manhood suffered any further harm. Just as I put Betsy back in her holster I was stopped abruptly in the hall. Unfortunately it appeared my Asian buddies had friends.

"Hey," I began with a smile, "let me guess. Wade and Maurice?" They didn't introduce themselves but the one who I think looked like a Maurice greeted me with a left hook that relieved me of my consciousness for a little while.

Chapter Six

Wade and Maurice really were not terribly hospitable. If I'm being totally honest, they were kind of jerks, really. I woke up on the sidewalk outside of the #1 Velvet Dragon warehouse a few hours later. Should I consider it a warehouse at this point? Nightclub? Gentlemen's Club? Dawn was beginning to break and it felt like it was breaking on my head.

"Son of a bitch," I muttered to myself as I attempted to drag myself to my feet. "That dude hit me like a brick." After stumbling a bit I was finally able to regain my balance. I looked around and found the Camaro sitting just where I'd left it. Dragging my sorry self across the parking lot to where the Camaro sat waiting for me was more of a challenge. I was about to slide myself into the seat when I saw the note pinned to the steering wheel.

Next time you won't be able to get up and walk away.

"Well that's not terribly pleasant. Who are you from?" I looked around to see if anyone was still watching. Not seeing anyone, I folded the note into my pocket before I fell into the driver's seat. I fired up the car and pointed it towards my office. The ride back to my office was very,

very long and very, very painful.

* * *

When I arrived at my office, the sight I walked into was something I wasn't happy to see.

"And the hits just keep coming."

Someone had kicked in my door and done a terrible job of rearranging my furniture. I surveyed my filing cabinets and desk, noting that they had been ransacked and my computer was missing. There were papers all over there place and all my information was on that laptop. I pulled out my iPhone and saw I had missed two calls. I poked at the screen and brought up the FindMyMac Locater App and saw that the last location my MacBook was turned on was here in my office. I hit the "Wipe" button, which would erase the entire laptop as soon it was turned on again and then swiped to see who had called. *Unknown* and a number I simply didn't recognize, but that happened all the time. I had two voicemails. I stood there weighing my options as to which was more important at that very moment... voicemail or the mess. The pounding in my head told me that I should sit down, so voicemail — you're the winner.

"Hey, it's me. You need to call me."

It's the detailed information that Linc leaves on his messages that I love the most. What a guy. Delete.

There was a pause of silence, so I pulled the phone from my ear to see it was from the mysterious *Miss Unknown.*

"You don't seem to get it," she started with a fast and furious tone. *"I told you to stay away and what do you do? You show up and ask for a lap dance?"* I was pretty sure that a lap dance wasn't all I was going to get from that

brunette. *"These guys are serious. I'm sorry I called you. Please forget I exist and stay away from that warehouse."* Again a pause before she finished softly with, *"Please, Lance."* Then she was gone.

She used my name and it sounded eerily familiar. I stared at my phone long enough for the screen to shut itself off while trying to place that voice. Before she just sounded like any young girl off the street... maybe a bit scared and confused, but just a young girl. But with those two words a bell went off and she sounded familiar. It was like hearing that voice in a cartoon that you just couldn't place. I just couldn't put a name to the voice. I decided the less I thought about it the quicker it would come to me. So I called Linc back.

"Yo, good buddy, how's it hangin'?" Trying to start off light and cheery, just like my day had been.

"You got a problem." That wasn't a question.

"Says you."

"No, says Ram Don Ming."

"Ram the what?" I'm nothing if not inappropriately amusing.

"You remember Soriano Mustafa?" I grunted ascent. "Mustafa is a pretty important guy. Owns people. Understand my meaning?" I grunted again. Sometimes you have to communicate with Linc on his level. "Mustafa isn't the head of the serpent. He's the front, the face. He's the guy who controls the minions. Ram Don Ming is the head. He's the big cheese."

"I love cheese."

Linc continued as if I hadn't spoken. "You asked about #1 Velvet Dragon and you sent me that license plate. Ram Don Ming owns #1 Velvet Dragon. Soriano Mustafa owns that Rolls. Ram owns Soriano. Get the connection?" I got it all right. That meant that Ram Don Ming must be the man behind that hooker heaven.

"What's #1 into? Girls?"

"Girls, guns, booze, powder, cars… whatever they can get their chopsticks into."

"Officially?"

"According to the IRS #1 Velvet Dragon is an importer of fine garments from China." The wheels were turning in my head. What does my mystery girl have to do with Ram Don Ming?

"This Ming fella, he a real shark?"

"Think great white. Biggest Asian on the East coast."

"Any chance he's running a high class brothel?"

"There's always a chance. Why?"

"I just got my pride hurt something awful by a couple of goons in what seemed to me to be a pretty high class whore house."

Grunt. Sometimes Linc didn't use his words very effectively.

"There were some pretty young girls there, Linc. I mean young. Not twenty-five young… *young* young! I need to find out what is going on in there. I need to get these girls out of that place before…"

"Lance," Linc shot the word out like a gun, "not every pretty young girl is Carolyn."

"I didn't say…" I started but I knew exactly what he meant. "It's not right, Linc."

"This world isn't right, Lance. You know that better than anybody I know. This world is a fucked up jigsaw puzzle that's missing two pieces and you ain't never gonna find 'em." I knew he was right but it didn't change how I felt.

"Yea, yea…" Time to shift the subject off my screwed

up life. "So any chance you could embellish on what you know about these sleezebags?"

"No." And with that he disconnected. I love Linc.

Ram Don Ming is a big hitter in the crime syndicate and this Soriano dude is connected to him. Soriano was at the warehouse today but I didn't see his Rolls tonight. What does that mean? Something? Nothing?

"Oh my Christmas!" came the squeal from Sally Ann in my doorway. "Lance, what happened?"

"I don't know Sally but good morning to you." I put on my best *it's cool* smile.

"Someone... they broke in and... look at this mess!"

I stared at Sally in her light blue skirt that sat just north of her perfectly formed knees, admiring how her pantyhose made her legs look so perfectly smooth.

"Lance? Hello?" She interrupted the beginnings of a lovely office-based fantasy. It had seriously been far too long since the last time I'd had some private time with a lady. "What were you thinking about? Seemed so far away." I flashed her my best *who me?* smile.

"Sorry, Sal, it's been a very long night."

"My word, Lance," she walked over to me and put her hand on my cheek, "what in the world happened to you? You look..." she had real concern in her eyes, "like you've been run over and then beaten on the head." She's incredibly perceptive. I never knew that about her.

"Sally, you have no idea how close you really are..." I shook my head once but was reminded how bad of an idea that was by the pulsating pain.

"You need to see a doctor, go to the ER!" she announced as if she was *Braveheart* himself. She grabbed my wrist and made the most valiant attempt to pull me to my feet.

"Sally, really. I'm fine. I've had worse. It was this bike messenger, I wasn't looking and he plowed into me. That's all." She let go and looked me over again.

"A bike messenger? You expect me to believe that?" She looked at me like I was a five year old. So I nodded my head like a child and smiled. "And you've had worse?" Her look was skeptical, laced with caring.

"Yup, I even had a doctor look at me. She fixed me up my boo boos and everything." Wasn't a complete lie. Nathalie was kind of, sort of, almost a doctor.

"But you have fresh blood on the side of your head." I do? I didn't notice. I reached up and felt the stickiness.

"It's nothing, I probably should be home on the couch is all, but look..." I gestured around my office. "Someone's gotta clean this up." She looked around with a frown on her lovely little face.

"I suppose so." She seemed to be retreating.

"As soon as I'm done here, BAM!" I slapped my hands together for effect and my pounding head made me immediately regret it. "I'm home on the couch. Promise!" It actually sounded like a great idea.

"Promise?" She cocked her head slightly and squinted.

"Promise." I hated lying to her.

"OK, you call me if you need me." I nodded in agreement with her and she was about to leave when I called out to her.

"Oh, hey, Sally. You dress nice — you into shoes?" She turned back to me with a crooked smile.

"Like an addict to crack. I mean, I am a woman, in case you hadn't noticed." I had and took another gander at those legs again.

"Sweet. So, what would you buy... Choo or

Louboutin?"

"Hands down, Louboutin!" she said with a bit of a twinkle in her eyes. "Not that I can afford them or anything, but Louboutin makes some sexy shoes and those red soles!" She gasped, "They are to die for!" She winked at me and resumed her clunking down the hall. Interesting.

I surveyed the mess left for me one more time and decided I needed to remedy my laptop situation before anything else. So I dialed my tech guru.

"Hey there, Lance. What's new in the detecting business?" Her pixie-like voice dripped through the phone.

"My office looks like a hurricane mated with a tornado right on top of my desk. It's not good. Detecting is what it is, my dear. How's things in geek land?"

"It is what it is, Sir Lance. I'm playing with the new Thunderbolt ports on my new MacBook. Ten gigabits! Super fast! You need one!"

"Giga-sweet! Funny you should mention a new MacBook. Gabby, I have a problem that I know you can solve." Gabby was a techno-geek of the highest order. She had her PhD from MIT and she was only twenty-seven. She had forgotten more about computers and technology than a classroom of comp sci majors knew. She had worked in the NSA right out of MIT and decided it just wasn't her cup of tea, so she quit and started her own technology consulting firm. Gabby had connections... her connections had connections... and most of those connections didn't officially exist. My tech-girl had connections with the highest government offices and clearances in all the dark corners. "My office was ransacked and wouldn't you know it, those bastards took my Mac!" I heard some furious click clacking of a keyboard.

"Done. I'll have a new one out to you for delivery

tomorrow and I'll activate FindMyMac as soon as we hang up. Did you remote wipe yet?"

"Yup."

"Excellent. I'll find it, Lance. FindMyMac has never failed me. Between that and Prey, we'll find it, take a picture of the unfortunate souls who took it and have that in the hands of law enforcement before the end of the day."

"You rock, Gabs."

"Office or apartment?"

"Is that a *my place or yours* invitation... I mean, we hardly know each other..."

"The MacBook, Lance." She tried to deadpan it, but I could hear the little giggle behind the words.

"Oh." I pretended to be confused. "Of course. My apartment would be lovely, I need some serious rest."

"OK, give me a shout when it gets there and I'll restore remotely from our off-site backup we have here."

After we hung up I rested a little bit easier knowing Gabby was on my Mac problem. I've lived through enough to know that you can't count on many people in your life. But I knew I could count on Gabby. In the end, I did what I promised. I suffered through bending over and standing up what seemed like a hundred times to clean up the torrent of papers and files all over the floor. But once the office was once again presentable I went home. When I walked into the apartment, Copper greeted me with his usual smile and tail wagging.

"Hey, furry buddy. I think I need to lay down for a bit." He cocked his head and stared at my face with a quizzical look. I swear he was asking me what happened to my head. My fur laden best friend looked me up and down and nodded at me before he trotted off to resume whatever it was he was doing. I kicked off my shoes and got horizontal on the couch.

And that was the end of the day for me.

Chapter Seven

The thumping of the bass and the glare of the lights was terribly distracting but I had her eyes locked on mine and I wasn't letting them go. Not this time, not again.

"Let's go, Carolyn."

"You let go of me, Carter. You let go of me now! You don't own me." She dangled her hand in front of my face. "There's no ring on this finger, you can't tell me what to do." My mind was racing, my blood was pumping and I couldn't get the image of her on that stage out of my mind. But there she was, standing in front of me in a pair of satin and lace panties with a matching bra. The lace negligee danced around her tanned skin giving the alluring illusion of cover and nudity at the same time.

"Carol, these people are dangerous. They don't screw around... is this the life you want? Come on... we need to get you out of here!" Her gaze was as fiery as ever and I could feel those baby blues penetrating the back of my skull like a laser. "Now, dammit!" I reached out and grabbed her arm.

"Let — GO!" she screamed and jerked her arm free of my grasp. I was reaching to regain my grasp when an extremely large black man that would make Ving Rahmes shudder blocked my view of Carolyn.

"Is there a problem here, muthfucka?" he growled in my direction.

"Fuck. You!" I spat back at him.

"I think you gonna find you getting the fuckin' round here... muthfucka!" He spat the words out at me.

"I think you might find me kicking your ass... mutha fucka." I had properly enunciated those last two words just at the time his big meaty hand found my jaw. My feet left the ground and I was sent reeling backward into a table.

Knock! Knock! Knock!

I was jolted awake from my horrible dream by the rapping at the door.

"What the... how...?" I sat up on the couch, looking around the room frantically. After a minute I had surmised I was in my apartment on my couch. And the only person here was the lovable fluff ball Copper trying to sleep under my desk on the far wall of the living room.

Bang! Bang! Bang! "Hello, delivery..." *Bang! Bang! Bang!* "FedEx! I need a signature!"

"OK. OK, geeez," I said, opening the door.

"Delivery, put the ring here please," the FedEx guy said.

"Put the what where now?"

"Sign here please?" His tone was that of an annoyed delivery man. I'm pretty sure that if you are wearing purple shorts, you aren't allowed to have an attitude.

"Oh, yea... of course." I shook my head to clear out the cobwebs, signed and took the box that held my lovely new MacBook Pro. After pulling it out of the box, I took a long moment to appreciate the sheer beauty of the enormous screen. Then I pushed the button and watched the pale grey Apple stare at me while it booted up. Once I had it hooked up to my wireless network, I dialed Gabby.

"Hey Lance, you ready for me?" she sang through the phone.

"You know just want I want to hear, Miss Gabby."

"OK, here goes. Make sure the machine stays on... 'k?"

"Will do. Hey, can I use it while the data restores? I have some research that needs doing..."

"Yea, sure can. Just don't shut down or restart for any reason. You'll see a green orb rotating in the menu bar at the top of your screen. Don't touch it. In an hour or so all your files will be back in your Documents folder."

A few minutes after we hung up I was on the Internet and looking up the name *Linda Sanders*. After about fifteen minutes I had a list of names and addresses from the Greater Philadelphia Area of people named Linda Sanders or L. Sanders. None of which matched the address Linda had written down for me. So I switched gears and searched for *Len Sanders*. Again there was a list of people none of which lived anywhere near the address scrawled down. I decided to look up the address instead of the person. I clicked on the *Address Lookup* link in my background search site and typed in the address 317 Broad Street #810, Philadelphia, PA. The site's screen changed to its *thinking* icon and then gave me a map showing the location of the address and the name *Larry Sanderson*. Coincidence? I don't believe in coincidences. It was time to give that address a little visit.

* * *

I felt like a moron as I drove around the block and read the big yellow and blue sign, *Packard*.

"Geez. It's the friggin' Packard Building." I should

have known it by the address. There's no way Linda and Lenny — at least not the Linda and Lenny I have become ever so vaguely acquainted with — could afford to live here. I pulled in the lot across the street, tipped the lot attendant heavily to *not* touch my car and found my way into the lobby. When I did I was surrounded by the opulent wood grain paneling on the walls and the plush carpeting that ran through the expanse of the large open lobby. I looked straight up as I lolled along and took in the fantastic chandeliers and green in-set ceiling that was bordered with white and gold accents. I practically tripped over the plush brown leather chairs in the middle of the lobby as I approached the deep walnut main desk.

"Can I help you, sir?" an older, grey haired black man in a green coat and black slacks asked very politely.

"Yea, hey, I'm looking for a... Linda Sanders? You wouldn't know which apartment she is in?" I flashed the Old Barker at him.

"Sir, I'm sorry. I'm not able to impart any information regarding the residents. If you would like to visit a resident, I can take their name and unit number and call up to them for you?"

"Number 810? Linda Sanders." The front desk guy clickety-clacked on his keyboard and shook his head.

"I'm sorry sir, there is no Linda Sanders in unit 810."

"No? Maybe it is under her husband's name? Lenny?" The clerk looked back at his screen and shook his head again.

"No, sir. I'm sorry, no Lenny Sanders either. Are you sure you are in the right building? There are many nice buildings in Philadelphia." I nodded my head absent-mindedly for a minute.

"Man, this is terrible." My face grew concerned. "You see, Linda gave me her address and I owe her money. I'm supposed to come by *today* to pay her back. It's going to put her in a real bind if she doesn't get it back and I'd just feel awful. You can understand that?" The old man nodded his head politely at me.

"That does sound terrible for Miss Linda."

"What to do, what to do?" I began tapping my fingers in a very irritating manner on the top of the desk while I glanced around nervously at other people milling about in the lobby.

"Sir, I... I wish there was something…" I smacked both hands down hard on the desk causing the nice old guy to jump in his seat.

"I've got it! It is under their son's name! Larry! Larry Sanderson!" My new best friend looked down at his screen and nodded affirmatively.

"Yes, sir. There is a Mister Larry Sanderson in unit 810." He reached over to pick up the desk phone. "I'll call up and announce you."

"Oh, no!" I put my hand on the phone. "Please don't. I… you see, I want to surprise Larry and Linda. You know, *Hey, look! I'm here with your money!*"

"Sir, I'm supposed to announce everyone who enters the building. It's standard operating procedure around here."

"How about you do me a solid?" I made a fist, hoping for a return bump. He stared at me. So I reached into my pocket and pulled a Ben Franklin out. Sliding it across the counter, "How about you do Ben a solid?" This time the old guy smiled, and buzzed me in.

* * *

The faux golden apartment numbers 8, 1 and 0 glared at me from the center of the door just below the peephole. I put my ear to what looked to be a freshly painted tan door. It went perfectly with the dark green carpet and pale green walls. After changing position on the door a couple of times I didn't hear anything inside the apartment. So I decided to knock on the door.

"Hello? Anyone home?" Nothing from inside. I tried the handle but it was locked but it was probably just like the Ben Franklin House, the doors were always locked from the outside. I slid a black leather case from my pocket and removed my lock pick. After a jiggle, a slide and a jerk to the left I felt the cylinder click. Ever so gently I turned the handle until I could feel the latch give. Pushing the door and listening and the same time, I entered the dark apartment. The door clicked quietly behind me and all I could see was the light leaking in from behind the drapes. It was so dark; all the windows must have been covered by drapes. I had just enough light to feel my way to one of the windows and pull the drapery open. When I turned and saw the apartment my head began nodding up and down all by itself. Just as I had thought, the *Sanders* weren't at all who they seemed to be. And I still wasn't sure where Janet Pence fit into the equation but she wasn't anyone's fairy godmother. The dark brown leather couch had to be straight off the showroom floor along with the matching armchair and recliner. Scanning from one side of the living room to the other, it had to be big enough to fit twenty people. I walked to the dark brown mahogany fireplace mantle to look at the framed pictures and saw the same chestnut haired boy smiling back at me in one. The next one had the spitting image of Lenny Sanders staring at me with his arm around the lovely Linda. Both were smiling with a peaceful and contented look on their faces. And finally at the other end of the mantel was a larger framed photo. I picked it up and looked at the little guy sitting happily on Linda's lap beneath a tree in what looked to be Washington Square Park.

"Guess I was wrong. You must have been blessed by the gods." This was clearly Linda's apartment and from what I could see, it was Lenny's too. But was Lenny really Larry? Or is there someone else name Larry and how do Linda and Sammy fit into the whole thing? I pulled out my iPhone and took a picture of the living room and added some shots of the pictures on the mantel.

Every once in a while I get a feeling. It is a feeling that tells me: *Hey, that's good. Pack it in, go home.* The problem is… I never pay any attention to that feeling. I had that feeling just before I opened the door to the bedroom that was just off the living room. I waltzed into the room and looked at the very expensive looking king size bed covered with a plush comforter and foo foo pillows. The thing that stood out the most about the room wasn't how expensive all the furniture was. The problem was how *lovely* it all was. I turned to look for a dresser and counted one with perfume bottles, a hairbrush and other feminine items strewn along the top. When I spun to look for the other dresser… it wasn't there. There was no armoire, highboy… nothing to indicate that another adult slept in this room. I walked into the adjoining bathroom, flipped on the light switch and was overwhelmed with the pink of it all. Pink tile, pink rug, pink towels with a big *L* monogrammed on them in a slightly lighter shade of pink. I felt my manhood trying to make a run for it. Much like that *go home* feeling... I should have listened.

I went back to the living room, now fairly confident that I had to figure out what the whole Lenny and Larry thing was and a little voice inside my head saying that Lenny and Larry are the same guy. But what did that say about Janet Pence and Linda Sanders... or is it Linda *Sanderson*? Unfortunately, I didn't have any more time to ponder that question before *my* lights went out.

Chapter Eight

My eyes flitted open but I couldn't see anything. I could feel that I was moving, in a car… maybe a minivan or something like that. Hard to tell from my current position. It seemed that I was face down in the back seat of something going very fast. The vehicle suddenly jerked to one side and the driver cursed wildly in Spanish as I tumbled to the floor. My head was splitting and I winced when it struck the back of the seat. The bad news was my hands were still bound behind me; felt like a zip tie. The good news was the my position had been adjusted just enough that I could see around me. I was in the backseat of a sedan of some kind with plush dark red seats. The kind that they would have put in older models of Lincoln Town Cars or Chevy Caprices. I looked at the back doors and saw the Chevrolet emblem, must be a Caprice.

"Where did heffe say to take him?" the passenger asked with a heavy Latino accent.

"We takin' him to the airport, homes," the driver with an equally heavy Latino accent answered.

"Niiiiice…" the passenger intoned, distracted by something outside the window. The driver reached over and hit something on the radio, bringing blaring Latin music from the speakers. If my head didn't hurt before, it did now.

Philadelphia Story by Bruce A. Sarte

Trumpets and drums were everywhere. The car took a corner hard and I slid about half a foot, mostly on my face, into a black bag of some kind. When I shook my head to free myself of the bag I noticed two things: one, my head was also bleeding into my eyes, and two, there was something hard in the black bag.

"Hey, what's dingo boy doing back there?" shouted the driver over the Salsa music.

"I dunno. Nothing!" Yelled the passenger, apparently not actually looking because I was suddenly very busy. I began working my mouth, trying to pull the bag open with my teeth. I was frantically gnawing and writhing at the bag when my tongue hit something nasty on the bag, causing me to reflexively gag and spit the bag out.

"Oh God..." I couldn't keep it in. I quickly realized how much noise I was making and tried to look up and see if my captors had heard me. There was no response from my new muchachos. When I returned to my bag-biting, I had made my way to the opening and started ferreting into the bag with my nose when it encountered something hard and cold. One sniff and I knew what it was...

"Betsy..." A big smile crept across my face as the plan formed in my head. Another glance up to see the head of the driver bobbing along to the beat and the passenger looked like he was almost asleep. I needed a little assistance. So I started screaming as loud as I could.

"Owwww! Damn it! Mother fucker, son of a bitch!" This immediately got their attention.

"Yo, man, what the fu... how'd he get on the floor, man?" the driver started yelling.

"Man, I don't... how the hell would I know! You the crazy muthfuckin' driver, yo!" the passenger retorted as if the driver was somehow blaming him.

"Oh, come on, dammit..." I started twisting and turning for effect. But it also helped push the Betsy further to the top of the bag and finally onto the floor.

"What's wrong with him?" the driver screamed and punched a button on the radio, stopping the infernal music.

"What am I? Doctor Killjoy? How the hell would I know, man?" Again, the passenger on the defensive. I continued to wriggle which pulled the zip tie a little bit loose — or maybe it was just digging into my skin more. I wasn't sure, but I knew it was mostly numb at this point.

"Well fuckin' do sumthin', man!" The passenger was now taking control of the situation. The driver didn't say anything but I felt the car sway to the side and screech to a halt. My body moved sideways and then slammed into the console.

"Assholes! Fucking... ahhhhhh!" I screamed even louder. But it really did hurt. "I'm gonna kick your asses all the way back to fucking Mexico, you beaner taco eating cocksuckers"

"Oh, that's it." The driver had apparently heard enough. The rather large Latino male jettisoned himself from the car and had the back door open in an instant. He stood there looking at me as if I were nothing more than a sack of potatoes. Meanwhile the passenger began to get out of the car, more slowly then the driver. I jerked my head backward grabbing a mouthful of that nasty black bag just as the driver grabbed one of my ankles, roughly yanking me from the car. I hit the pavement hard with the bag spilling out behind me.

"You calling me a bean eater? I'm gonna kick your ass, gringo." And he did. Several kicks with the toe of his boot landed squarely in my stomach. Suddenly this plan didn't seem like a good idea... until his buddy came around.

"Yea, grin, muthafucka!" He grabbed my collar and yanked me up to my feet. He was big and strong just like his buddy. But he was slow. He wound up to sink a right roundhouse into my head but I struck out at him with a head butt right to the bridge of his nose. His face exploded in a gushing fountain of blood and pain. When my right foot connected with his groin, he was already screaming in agony. Now I'm pretty sure he was one bad moment away from losing consciousness, so I gave it to him with a kick to the face. His buddy, the driver, must have been stunned because he didn't make a move. I turned on him and landed a left sidekick to his chest that sent him reeling back into the trunk of the car. A quick look at the passed out Latino and I spotted a knife in his back pocket. I ran over, carefully squatted down retrieving the knife about two seconds before the driver regained his balance. I had just began sawing away at the zip tie when he began advancing on me.

"Go ahead, try that cheap shit on me again." Now the driver produced a knife not unlike the one I had in my hands. Problem was, mine was behind me.

"What?" I said. "Like this?" And started the kick again but pulled back as his hand swiped the knife through the air. I spun on my heel and fell to the ground swiping his legs out from under him, sending his two-hundred-plus-pound frame to the ground... hard. I was back on my feet working the zip tie again until it snapped. My hands were now free and I moved my feet toward Betsy. I lunged to where Betsy had fallen, retrieved my gun only to be grabbed by my feet again and yanked backward. He wasted no time putting his boot firmly into my skull sending my senses on a roundabout trip to hither and yon. I instinctively rolled into a ball and he continued to kick at my back. It hurt but wasn't a game ender. Betsy had jumped from my hands but

I saw the she was just an arm's length away. I reached out, clutched the gun just as his boot came down on the ground missing my hand by the tiniest of margins. He recovered and tried to bring his knee down into my shoulder but I quickly rolled and brought Betsy's barrel to bear on my driver friend.

"You'd better stop and think outside the bun on this one, mijo. We can do this the easy way or the hard way," I began in my best Dirty Harry impression. "Putting two into you is the easy way." Staring him down the Betsy's sleek barrel I noticed something incredibly familiar about him. It was Sleeves from the #1 Velvet Dragon warehouse.

"C'mon, man," Sleeves started putting his hands out in a pleading gesture, "we just tryin' to do our job, man. You know?"

"You're the guys from the club. I'd know that disaster of a tattoo job anywhere." He glanced self-consciously at his arms.

"Hey man, these cost me a lotta coin, bro… don't…"

"Shut up." I stood and took a step in his direction to emphasize my point. "This isn't the part where you get all self-righteous. This is the part where you're going to tell me what the hell is going on here and why you were in Linda's apartment. Or I start picking out spots on your body to see how good my aim really is." Apparently I wasn't imposing enough, because Sleeves started walking toward me slowly with a smile on his face.

"Man, you ain't gonna cap me. Hell no, you ain't." He stopped three steps from me with his hands still raised about halfway.

"No? And why is that?" I growled as I cocked Betsy.

"Because I know everything you need to know, brutha. Yea, I do. It's all right here!" He started jabbing

68

Philadelphia Story by Bruce A. Sarte

his finger into his head.

"Doesn't do shit for me if it's up there, mijo. Why did you grab me from Linda's apartment?"

"Linda? Who the fuck is Linda?" He started backing away toward the car and I noted movement form the guy on the ground. "I thought you'd be more worried about Tinker Belle then whoever this Linda bitch is... whateva man...." The guy on the ground started to his feet.

"Get the fuck down, taco-boy!" He looked up at me, then at his buddy. "You got three seconds. One..." Now they both looked at each other and in an instant, Sleeves was on the driver's seat throwing the car into gear as the other guy jumped into the back seat. I squeezed off two rounds that found their way into the rear driver's side door but the lime green Caprice roared away seemingly unaffected, leaving me standing in the middle of the street, bleeding and holding a smoking gun. I took a minute to take in my surroundings and realized that the black bag was on the pavement. After a moment of rooting around I found my iPhone underneath some newspapers. A quick phone call and Linc was on his way to pick me up.

Chapter Nine

"You gonna be OK?" Linc asked through his usually clenched teeth. I opened my eyes just enough to see the deep concern on his face. That is to say I think the side of his mouth twitched as he spoke.

"I think I'm going to live…"

"Yea, but it's not going to be a good life." Lincoln was nothing if not brilliantly amusing. Through my blurry vision I think the side of his mouth raised up just a notch. Linc's version of falling down laughing.

"As if it were good before…" I was about to close my eyes when there was a soft knocking sound coming from the door.

"Want me to get that?" Linc asked with his attention focused on the door.

"Ya know what, maybe you should. I'm not the most popular guy in Philly these days." Lincoln grunted and crossed the room to the door. I put my head down and closed my eyes trying to relax and make the throbbing go away.

"What?" the female voice came from the door. "Well, can I…"

"I don't think that's a good idea, miss." Linc replied.

"But I'm a doctor. If Lance is hurt he needs to see a

doctor," she implored Lincoln to let her in.

"Stay here." He crossed the room back to me. "Lady says she's a doctor. Kind of looks like Marisa Tomei. She wants to come in."

"I don't know any doctors." I rolled over and put my face in the pillow of the couch. "Whoever it is, tell her to come back later."

"Lance!" I heard the voice come from the door.

"Wait." I looked at Linc. "Did you say she looked like Marisa Tomei?"

"Yea," Linc grunted out, "kinda…"

"It's me, Nathalie. I came to say hi." I bolted upright and regretted it before I could process the thought associated with the action.

"Oh, yea, come on in. I'm sorry." I started to get up and fell back down onto the couch. My head felt like I was stuck in a tube of water. I put my hand on my forehead. "Linc, she's OK. Let her in."

"Alright, but I'm out of here." And before I could say anything else, I opened my eyes and saw that Linc Diesel was gone. Fortunately for me, his rough and tough exterior was replaced by the slender attractive image of Nathalie Tomei.

"Oh my God, Lance, what happened to you?"

"It's nothing," I waved my hands in the air to try and dispel her concern, but the look on her face didn't change.

"Lance, sit still." She held my eye lids open for a second. "You have a concussion. Lie back and stay still." She went into the kitchen and returned with a glass of water for me. "Here, drink. You have to stay hydrated and relax." She pulled up a chair closer to the couch and sat. I drank and put my head down on the pillow.

"I'm telling you, it hurts like hell," I admitted with

my eyes closed.

"What happened, Lance? I've seen you twice now and both times your head has been bleeding. That's not good." She looked me up and down, taking stock of the situation. "What exactly do you *do* all day?"

"I'm a detective. I find things that people either lost or don't know exist. Sometimes..." I sighed and looked away for a moment. "Sometimes things happen and people get hurt while I'm finding those things."

"What kind of things are you looking for?" Nathalie produced a wet rag and placed it on my forehead.

I chuckled. "I've looked for everything from lost dogs to lost kids to lost love..."

"People certainly are very careless with the things they are supposed to care about, aren't they?" I opened my eyes again and saw her face morph from concern to dark. The blue in her eyes seemed to change two shades darker right before my eyes.

"Yea, I guess they are. I went to the Packard Building thinking I was looking for one thing and the next thing I knew it was obvious I didn't know anything." She nodded her head and stared at me for what seemed like forever. My eyes got heavier with each passing flutter of her eyelids and I found myself slowly drifting off to sleep with the image of her slightly crooked smile burned on my retinas.

* * *

The opening chords to *Smoke on the Water* came screaming from my iPhone and shook me out of my slumber. I love that ringtone. I rolled off the couch and crashed to the floor in my feeble attempt to answer the call, but my phone wasn't on the coffee table. I decided it might be in my best interest to lie still on the floor before attempting to get up. I then, very slowly, picked up my head only to be greeted by a cold wet nose in my eye followed my a warm, wet tongue to my nose.

"Hey Copper, old pup, how you doing buddy?" I pushed up to my knees, pulled my favorite ball of fur into my lap and began petting him furiously. Suddenly he burst from my grasp and bounced to and fro, then ran in a circle barking before eventually finding his tennis ball. He stormed across the living room, fur-a-flying and threw the ball into my belly. I looked down at the ball, now on the floor, then back up at Copper who was now panting like a ravenous hound with his tail wagging a mile-a-minute. I looked him straight in the eye and he stopping panting but the tail continued to flail in his hindquarters. Then, after a long pause, I tossed the ball down the hall and watched him go bounding after it. I took this opportunity to look around the living room and note that I did not see my fair Nathalie anywhere. Getting to my feet, I grabbed the glass of water from the table took a long drink before making my way into the kitchen. I was about to refill my glass when I noticed a pocketbook on my kitchen table. It was black and left open so one could see inside. When I saw the black business card with gold print and an embossed red dragon on the front, my heart skipped a beat.

#1 Velvet Dragon
South Philadelphia

I was reaching for the pocketbook to get a better look when the bathroom door down the hall opened.

"Oh, Lance, you're up. I was starting to worry a bit..." Nathalie said as she walked down the hall, hands behind her head putting her hair into a ponytail. I watched it bob back and forth toward me.

"Yea, my phone was ringing but I missed the call. Not sure where it is actually." She came up to me, buried her face in my chest and hugged me tight.

"You look better," she said with her face muffled by my shirt. "I was worried."

"I'm feeling much better." I placed my hands tentatively around her back and embraced her ever-so-lightly. With her head resting on my chest, my gaze returned to the pocketbook and the business card. What did she have to do with #1 Velvet? Was she a dancer? Maybe she was paying for school by stripping? Or... hooking? She certainly had the body for it... and it was currently warmly pressed up against mine. Nathalie squeezed me and pushed her hips firmly into my groin in the most pleasant way. I closed my eyes and thoughts of #1 Velvet Dragon drifted away. Nathalie's body wriggled slightly and I felt warm lips on my neck punctuated by a gentle lick. Reflexively my head tilted down to meet her inviting mouth and we kissed. It was warm and comforting. It was one of those kisses when your lips interlock and stay that way without moving. It was familiar yet new and we both easily fell into it. When we finally parted I heard her gasp just a little bit.

"Oh," she said, "Lance, I..."

"Shhh," I put my finger to her lips, "don't." The gaze locked and we held it until the Deep Purple's chords rang out once again. Reality came hurdling back to me. A quick look at the clock told me it was 12:45 in the morning. I broke the embrace and raced into the living to locate my phone. I picked it up on the third rendition of the opening to *Smoke on the Water*.

"Hello?" I hadn't noticed the number.

"Lance?" the now-familiar female voice asked tentatively.

"Yea, yea... I mean, yes, it's me." I was a little out of breath and could feel my head begin to throb just a bit from the exertion.

"Can you help me?" she said in a quiet monotone. There was almost no emotion behind it whatsoever.

"I don't know. You keep calling but you never say anything." I tried not to sound desperate but I knew my desire to help her was creeping through. Nathalie came into the living room out of the corner of my eye. "How can I help?"

She was quiet, no response for a solid minute but I didn't push. Then with a thoughtful tone she said, "I'm in trouble, I need help... I need your help. They... I need help."

"I want to help, sweetheart, but I don't know what you need..."

"Come, help me... I'm hiding. They're going to.... I'm scared!" There was an urgency creeping into her voice and it kicked my protective streak into overdrive. I looked at Nathalie. She was watching me but not reacting at all to my glance.

"Where are you? I will come right now!" I visually searched the room for my holster. "Tell me where, I'll keep you safe." Nathalie take a step closer to me with her head cocked slightly.

"Come to the boat... the restaurant..." There was noise in the background. "Someone's coming — I have to hide." There was more rustling and I was about to speak when she fired off the next line. "You know where it is, Lancelot, hurry!" And then line went dead.

"I know where it is…" I mumbled staring at the lock screen picture of Copper sitting in front Independence Hall staring off into the distance as if he were watching something. Maybe he was watching my mystery caller by the boat. The one that I know where it is, only I don't…

"You know where what is, Lance?" Nathalie asked.

"The boat?" I answered weakly, putting my phone in my pocket.

"What boat?" Nathalie was suddenly in front of me.

"That's the problem. I don't know. But she said I'd know… only I don't. How am I supposed to know? I don't even know who she is…" I stared down into Nathalie's face hoping for some understanding, but instead her eyes grew probing and all I got were more questions.

"She's on a boat? Where?"

"I just told you I don't…" But then like a slap in the face what she said echoed in my mind… *you know where it is, Lancelot.* The voice, so young and familiar… and she called me Lancelot. "I know where she is." I grabbed Betsy and my car keys from the table and started for the door.

"Oh no, mister. You aren't going anywhere," Nathalie said firmly with a hand on my chest.

"I have to… she needs me," I implored her.

"You can't go out, you have a concussion and I'm still thinking something in there," she poked at my chest, "is broken. Or maybe it's up here?" She tapped my head lightly.

"As much as I enjoy you touching me, I have someone… she knows who I am, she called *me* for help. There's a reason my phone rang." And my Jesus complex kicked in as I side-stepped Nathalie for the door.

"Where are you going?" she yelled after me.

"Lance?"

"The Moshulu!" I answered without looking. I heard the door slam in the wake of my hasty departure.

Chapter Ten

The information and details danced around in my head created a very loud combination of clutter and white noise in my head. The unholy combination was almost as loud as the 427 roaring inside my Camaro as I pushed the accelerator even harder into the floorboard. The tires squealed as I cut through the circle under the Ben Franklin Bridge towards Columbus Boulevard. I spun the wheel and fishtailed around the corner roaring toward The Moshulu. It had been a very long time since I was here last and the memories I had were not pleasant. As the engine screamed past the Maritime Museum the rain began to fall lightly onto the windshield but I didn't kick on the wipers. No time for wipers… I had to get to The Moshulu — now. It was after one in the morning now and the restaurant would be closed now. I remember reading in the paper that it had re-opened for business a few years back but I never ate there. I turned the corner and slammed on the breaks, my car now sitting facing the dark ship ebbing with the roll of the current on the river.

It had indeed been a long time. I replayed that phone call from Lindsey in my head. The desperation in her voice still filled me with the urgency to save her little girl. I killed the engine and got out of the car, frantically searching for signs of life somewhere on or around the ship. The old warehouse had been refurbished into a Pier One. Ironic, eh?

I bolted toward the gangplank and leapt over the chain in one swift motion. Without stopping, it took three long strides before I was on deck. The wind hit my face hard and pushed my eyelids closed. I regained my composure and quickly scanned the parking lot that I'd just come from. No cars or signs of life. I turned back to the deck of the large ship. I scanned and saw no movement, no signs of anyone or anything. I slowly started toward the bow, where the deck bar was located. There were about twenty tables seemingly randomly placed in the general area of the bar. The area was dark, the only light coming from the Ben Franklin Bridge and surrounding buildings in that were off in the distance. Everything in the seating area looked as I would expect it to look. As my eyes got to the bar I noticed there was one bar stool that had fallen to the deck, near the end. As if someone accidentally knocked it over as they went around the bar to get behind it. Maybe to hide. I squinted my eyes hard to try and enhance my ability to see behind the dark bar but it didn't help. Why do I do that? It never makes me see any better. I crossed the seating area toward the fallen stool, hoping to be able to get a better look into the blackness that permeated the bar-back.

"Jennifer... are you here?" I called out in a firm but quiet voice. "Jenny?" There was no answer. I continued to move toward the bar. I was still not able to make anything out beyond the occasional flash of a headlight from Columbus Boulevard glaring off a bottle. Most bars have a mirror on the bar-back, but this one didn't seem to. I was about fifteen feet from the bar when a sudden swishing sound made me stop dead in my tracks. Was it the sound of clothes rubbing against the floor? But then it came again, hard and fast and I could tell it was nothing more than the water slamming against the hull of the boat. I let my breath out but then jumped and whirled at the sound of a car horn on Columbus Boulevard.

"Son of a bitch…" I muttered, my heart now pounding in my chest. It was chilly out, but I still had to wipe the sweat off my brown. I turned back toward the bar and found myself staring into the same deep, green eyes that I had been staring into at the #1 Velvet Dragon.

"Lancelot…" she practically whispered.

"I should have known… how didn't I know? You look just like your mother."

She broke her gaze and her face drifted toward the Delaware. "My mother…" Her voice was ethereal and wispy. "I miss my mother," she stated simply.

"Jennifer, where have you been? I… they took you… and…" She put her hand up without looking at me.

"I don't…. I can't hear about that now." Suddenly she seemed a mile away even though she was only a few feet from where I stood. I didn't know what to say… or if I should say anything so I just let the sound of the passing cars fill the void for a few minutes.

"Jennifer?" I took a step toward her but then she started talking, so I stopped.

"They're back, Uncle Lance… they are after me again. I thought… it was over but then they were just there one night."

"What are you talking about? Who is back?" I cut the distance between us in half. Almost as if she was taking her cues from a script she spun and met me half way.

"The men who had me, the ones who took me. They're back. They weren't here before." There was a deep-rooted fear in her voice. "He… that man. The one with the gun. He was in my apartment. One night I woke up and he was standing at the end of my bed. Smiling with his ugly yellow teeth."

"He was in your apartment? What happened?" My voice cracked just a bit.

"He pointed his gun..." The squealing of tires and flashing of headlights interrupted Jennifer. We both jerked our heads toward the parking lot. "They found me... they followed you!" she screamed, and before I could respond, she ran towards the door to the restaurant that led below deck. As quickly as I could, I gave chase. By the time I reached the steel door it had already slammed shut. I stopped to look back toward the parking lot and saw several men congregating at the base of the gangway. I could hear their voices but couldn't hear what they were saying. I tried to get a look at them but there were two very large men blocking my view of the others. Shooting through the door, I decided giving chase to Jenny was more important than taking stock of our new arrivals. As soon as the door slammed I was engulfed by the darkness within. I pulled out my iPhone and loaded the Flashlight app. Pointing it straight ahead I could see restrooms on the left and what looked like a railing for stairs straight ahead. As I began to make my way toward the railing I heard steps thumping from below.

"Jennifer?" I yelled but got no answer. When I reached the railing and pointed my iPhone over the edge I was able to see a grand staircase that extended down into what looked to be a beautiful lobby. The stairs were framed by stunning handcrafted wooden banisters capped with giant lion's heads that looked to be heavier than a fully grown person. The lions were staring off into the darkness but on the other side of the far lion I could see dimly lit emergency lighting coming through what looked to be beautifully etched glass. From where I was standing this place was immaculate. The sound of a door slamming shut somewhere on the lower level pulled me out of my moment of admiration.

"Feet don't fail me now," I muttered to myself as I skittered down the stairs and used the lion head as a pivot point to shoot me off down the hall toward the sound. The hallway down here had rope lighting along the walls so I could at least see where I was heading without concern for running into a wall or off a ledge. I came to a stop staring at a painting of Admiral David G. Farragut frowning at me. End of the hallway. The lights jumped to life all around me at the same time a chorus of footfalls began to sing above me.

"Shiiiit," I muttered as I looked at the ceiling above me.

"You," a Middle Eastern voice commanded, "look in there. You two, over there and you two, downstairs." There was no reply but apparently they didn't move fast enough because then the voice barked, "Now!"

I began to look left and right but just as I took a step back I hear a soft tapping on the glass to my right. When I looked, a glass door peeked open at me and fell shut on its own. I decided *this* was a good direction and slipped my way into that room and behind the false security offered by the glass. The room was still dark but for a wall sconce giving off a soft creamy light that illuminated a circle around it and that was all. I could see bookshelves filled with leather bound volumes and a small wooden desk in the middle of the room. It had a lamp, some papers strewn about, a computer monitor, and the top of a brunette head staring at me intently.

"Over here," she hissed at me and ducked back down. When I slid down onto the floor she looked at me sideways. "You're awfully slow for a private detective."

"Hey, I'm almost..." But she cut my off with an elbow to the ribs. I went quiet and rubbed my side. Jenny was sneaking a peek around the side of the desk but then returned her gaze to the wall behind us.

"Jenny, it is only a matter of time before they find us here." I whispered just loud enough for her to hear. She didn't answer, only nodded her head. "There has to be a way below this level into the hull of the ship. We can go below and wait them out there."

"Wait them out? You can't get us out of this?" she asked, a bit incredulous. I began to speak but stopped myself.

"Well... wait. Maybe I can." I pulled out my iPhone and pushed Linc's contact number. It rang once.

"Yea," was all he said.

"Linc, need an assist here, pal." I could hear the goons finally making their way down the stairs.

"Where and how many?"

"Moshulu and maybe eight or ten guys. I didn't get a really good look."

"Is that all?" He paused for effect, I assume. "Be there in fifteen. Stay alive." And he was gone.

"Did you call in the calvary?" Jenny asked, pushing herself under the middle of the desk, her hands shaking just a bit. I could tell she'd become a tough girl over the years but that scared little girl was still in there.

"Yea, honey," I said reassuringly. "Something like that."

"How many are there? Do they have guns?" The shaking was starting to spread.

"I don't know, maybe ten of them. Yes, I'm pretty sure they brought guns." This certainly wasn't going to be a knife fight. "We need to keep quiet. Not raise suspicion."

"Right," she said, nodding her head. "Quiet." She had pulled her knees up to her chest under the desk so her long black skirt fell around her like a cocoon. I could only see the whiteness of her face from the eyes up behind her knees. Then the footsteps starting getting closer. I could hear the goons coming. Not too far off I heard a door open and close. A moment later the footsteps moved back into the hall and a door closed. The steps went thumpity-thump and another door opened. This time I could hear them enter the room next to ours and there was a little bit of discussion. The goons didn't spend more than a minute in that room before they were back out into the hall, presumably coming to this office. The feet approached the door and pushed it open slowly. Now I could feel them entering the room. It would only be moments before they came around the desk and saw me. I reached into my jacket and felt Betsy there beside me. I pulled her out as slowly and quietly as possible.

"Over here," one of them said with what might have been a Chinese accent to his fairly clean English. The other pair of footsteps crossed the room. It sounded like they were by the table underneath the sconce.

"What the hell is this?" the one with a Latin accent replied. I'd know that voice anywhere, it was Sleeves. I could feel my blood begin to boil and I shifted my weight back into the desk to block their view of Jennifer.

"Wait, shhh," the Chinese goon said. "Did you hear that?"

"Hear what, poncho?" Sleeves said.

"That," the Chinese guy said matter-of-factly. Crap,

they heard me move.

"Yea, I heard that." I put both hands on Betsy's grip and prepared to whirl and fire. Then the two moved, quickly, through the door and were gone. I was dumbfounded. Where did they go? The door slammed behind them and I could hear their feet scrambling up the stairs and there was frantic yelling. Then I heard a thump and a thud. I grabbed Jennifer's arm and pulled her out from the desk. She pulled back a little but I shot her a quick *move now*! look and she followed me out of the office and down the hall. By the time we reached the staircase I didn't hear anyone moving upstairs. Then I heard slow and steady footfalls. They were moving away from us. Then abruptly, they stopped and began quickly coming our direction.

"Shiiiiit!" I said, just a little too loud, and pulled Jennifer across the lobby and away from the stairs. We pushed through saloon style doors and made our way into the bar area. As soon as the doors swung shut behind us, we were engulfed in a chasm-like darkness.

"This way!" Jennifer said as she pulled me into the darkness without even looking twice. She weaved a couple of times before slowing and finally stopping. I still couldn't see what she was doing, but I heard a key go into a lock and a door swing open. "In here…" She beckoned me to follow. When I did, she slowly closed the door behind me and I heard a lock click.

"Where are we?" I asked while looking around. There was light coming from one porthole that dimly illuminated what can only be described as a cramped space. I could see the outline of what looked like a chest of two drawers, a small table with a mess of papers on it and a bed on the floor against the wall of the ship.

"We are in my house... err... apartment? Or what do

they call them on boats, cabin? Yea, that's it... it me cabin, matey!" she said with no mirth whatsoever in her voice.

"So, you live here? On the boat?" I asked with a note of incredulity.

"Umm... yea, I live here on the boat. It's not much but it's home?" She paused and I could see her look around. "I know it sucks... but... after Mr. M was standing at my bed, I had to get out of there. I couldn't stay." Jennifer wrapped her arms around herself and flopped down on her bed. The lights from the parking lot silhouetted her frame making her look surreal and fragile. She reached up and wiped at her face at what I could only guess was a tear.

"Mr. M? As in the #1 Velvet Dragon Mr. M?"

She threw her arms away from herself. "Yup, the very same. He's the low-life who showed up at my apartment and dragged me to that dressed up whore house."

"What happened?"

"That night he put a gun to my head and told me to come with him. So I did. I... I.." She sniffled. "I didn't know what else to do. He put me in the back of this car and the next thing I knew we were at this dumpy warehouse. He pushed me inside and all of a sudden I was in this posh club. It was totally decked out, I mean there was red velvet everywhere, and sparkly gold and flashy things... it was intoxicating." She paused and then stood up. "His goons pushed me into one of those rooms... in the back. You know." I put my hands up.

"Yes, I remember it all now... a bit too clearly." I rubbed at my jaw.

"Yea, umm..." She stumbled awkwardly over her words. "I didn't really know that was you and all... I mean, you looked familiar but when I'm doing *that* I don't really look at the guys. You know?"

I felt my face go flush with embarrassment and was so glad it was dark. "Let's not... tell me what else happened." My phone buzzed in my pocket; I had a text.

"They threw me in one of those rooms and Mr. M told me that I had no choice, to work in the club or he'd... he'd do... really, terrible, awful things to me. I mean, he told me what he'd do and it..." She stopped.

"It's OK. So M kidnaps you and makes you... what? Dance? Strip? Hook?"

"No!" She was emphatic in her denial. "I did not sleep with anyone!"

"Hey." I put my hands up in defense. "I'm just trying to figure out what's going on and how I can help you. You call me a couple of times, you hang up on me a couple of times, I got my ass kicked a couple of times... these aren't good things and quite frankly I could do without the ass kicking part." I walked up to her, taking her cold and shaky hands into mine. "Jenny, I was always there for your mom—and I'm here for you. You called and as soon as I figured out it, I came. What I need from you now is... what is going on here?"

"I don't know!" she insisted, throwing my hands away from her. "They came after me, told me if I didn't dance and strip, they wouldn't kill me, they'd torture and rape me and do awful things. So I did it. I danced, I took my clothes off and shook my body for them because I was scared... and I am still scared!" My phone buzzed in my pocket again. "Then one night... last week... Mr. M grabbed me as I was coming in and asked me where the information was. I told him I had no idea what he was talking about but he pushed me down and insisted that I knew. He told me I had one week to give him the information or he'd make it messy. I don't even know what that means!" She was practically screaming now.

"And you have no idea, no clue what *information* he is looking for?" She shook her head, reached into her shirt and pulled out that golden key she had from years ago. She began playing with it nervously. "I think we need to make sure you are safe." I looked around the room. "And I'm not sure this is safe."

"I know one of the bartenders who works here. He was..." she turned away, "one of the guys from the club who was really nice to me. When I told him I needed a place to stay, he let me stay here."

"From the club? How would a bartender get into the club?"

"I don't know, but Roger was just so nice. He seemed like he had money." She shrugged. "Maybe he owns the boat, I don't know. I don't care as long as M doesn't know."

"I hate to tell you this, Jenny, but I think he knows now. Those guys here tonight, they were M's guys." She turned back and looked at me with questions written in her eyes.

"How do you know these guys are from Mister M?"

"I just know... well, I mean I knew one of them from a little altercation we had earlier in the day. You have to trust me, these guys that showed up here tonight are after you *and* me."

My words seemed to affect her. Her face changed, grew softer. "Lancelot, why were you so... what did my mom mean to you?" The question hit me like a linebacker from my blindside. I never saw it coming.

"I... Lindsey... we had..." And the my phone started to play *Hell's Bells*. It was Linc, so I answered it. "Linc, buddy... we're in the bar, hiding in the front room. It's..."

And then there was a pounding on the door. I walked over, pulled it over and saw my reflection in Lincoln Diesel's reflective sunglasses. It would seem to be a bad idea to wear such glasses at four in the morning but not to Linc. He wore those glasses almost everywhere.

"Let's go."

"Who the hell is that?" Jennifer exclaimed.

"That's Lincoln Diesel, he's my partner... of sorts." I turned and responded with a smile. "That's who I called before."

Linc looked from me to Jennifer. "Now."

"But what about the goon squad?" she asked.

"I created a diversion." Linc said, put a toothpick in his mouth, turned and walked back out through the bar.

"A diversion?" She had a very confused look on her face.

"Well, you heard the man and you really don't want to know. Shall we?" Jennifer and I followed Linc out of The Moshulu.

Chapter Eleven

"If they didn't follow you then how did they know where we were?" Jennifer kept insisting. The morning sunlight brought out some underlying brown highlights in her otherwise raven hair.

"There's no way they followed me. I was there for almost fifteen minutes before those cars rolled in. They would have been there before then. There's something else going on here. There's *someone* else involved."

"Who?" she asked.

"What do we know about that doctor girl you're all fuzzy with?" Linc scratched out.

"Nathalie? How would she be involved? She wouldn't even know me if it weren't for the accident."

"Accident?" Linc asked.

"Yea, bike messenger took me out on Chestnut. Laid me out flat, Nathalie helped me up, even took her shirt off." I smiled. "They were nice."

"*They?*" Jennifer asked.

"I mean she… she was nice," I coughed out a cover up. "My point is it was purely coincidental that we even met.

"The May-December thing doesn't have you concerned?" Linc asked looking over his shades at me.

Philadelphia Story by Bruce A. Sarte

"The what? May... what?? I'm September at the worst man, come on."

"I'm not kidding. A girl like that just falling for you like this? And now the Asian mafia mixed up with a strip club slash brothel that just happens to be after a girl you know?" Linc stood up. "I know what you think of coincidences, Lance."

"Yea," I rubbed my face in my hands, "there's no such thing."

"What about this whole Sanders thing? Any connection there?"

I thought about Linc's question for a moment. "Other than being jumped in Linda's apartment I don't see the connection. There's something that isn't right about it. It stinks from here to South Broad Street but I don't see any connection to Jennifer."

"Wait!" Jennifer said. "That name sounds so familiar to me..."

"Linda Sanders?" I threw the name back out there hoping hearing it again would jostle something inside her.

"I know a Linda. She's blonde." My ears perked up at that revelation. "Yea, Sanderson."

"Sanderson?" I questioned. "You know a Linda Sanderson?"

"Yea, blonde hair down to here," she motioned about halfway down her back, "blue eyes, about this tall?" She moved her hand up accordingly.

I nodded. "Yea, big rack?"

Jennifer looked disgusted with me but nodded her head anyway. "She was a dancer at #1 but I haven't seen her in like... I don't know, a week maybe?" Jennifer sipped at her coffee. I went over to my table and pulled the pictures out. Walking back to Jennifer, I flashed them.

"Any of these look familiar to you?"

"Yea, that's Lenny and Linda and their son. What's his name... oh, I don't know. But yea, that's them." She was nodding.

"Son of a bitch," I murmured.

"What?" Linc asked.

"I've been set up. This whole thing. I need a friggin' drink."

"Set up how?" Jennifer asked but I didn't really hear her.

"The goons... they lead me on with a missing boy and pretty face. They knew I'd go to the apartment. They set me up to nab me and then..." I let that hang out there for a minute and the turned my gaze to Jennifer. "But how does that tie into you, my dear?"

"I..." she looked at me, then at Linc and then back to me, "don't know?" She was unsure of herself. Made me think she knew *something*. I decided to go after that *something*.

"There has to be something there, Jenny. Have they mentioned me to you...? Do they know there is a connection between you and me? We know they found you. We know they are trying to get *something* from you. We know they found me but I'm not sure why."

"You're in the way of that *something*," Linc contributed in his usual monotone. I looked over at him but he was looking out the window.

"I suppose you have something there, my flat-topped friend," I said, nodding. Linc reached up and ran his right hand over his closely cropped hair.

"So," Linc continued, "it seems to me it is time to figure out what that *something* is." Sometimes he was a master at stating the obvious. I nodded my head in

92

agreement.

"And just how do we do that...?" Jennifer asked, flopping back on the couch.

"Did you dance last night?" I asked.

"Yea, of course... if I don't dance he sends his goons looking for me. It is... well, I guess until last night it *was* the only way I could keep my hole in the ship a secret. Now they know where I live so that's up the crapper."

"Up the crapper?" Linc looked confused.

"Tonight you go to work. Go and see Ram Don Ming when you get there. Linc and I will have your back."

"I don't know where he is, how am I supposed to find him?"

"Tell that bunny girl at the front you have what he wants. She'll do the rest."

* * *

Linc and I were parked a half a block away from #1 Velvet Dragon's joint. Just far enough to not arouse suspicion but close enough that we could see the front door. It was a clear evening on the south side of Philadelphia. The sun had begun its slow descent into the western sky but was still giving off a warming orange glow.

"Where is she?" Linc growled from the passenger seat of the Camaro. The top was actually up tonight.

"Patience, my good man, patience. We need her to go to work just like she would on any other day." Linc grunted his understanding. After ten more minutes the sun had receded behind the Philadelphia skyline and Jennifer walked up to the steel door and stopped.

"Come on, Jenny. Just go in," I muttered. She looked around nervously and then seemingly steeling herself, she opened the door and went in.

"OK, show time." I pulled my iPhone out and opened the FindMe app that my favorite tech-girl, Gabby, had written just for me. After a moment the app brought up a top-down view of Philadelphia. It thought about it for another moment before moving to South Philly and zooming in. It paused again, flashing at me slightly before focusing above South Broad Street and zooming in on the top of the warehouse.

"Working?" Linc gritted out his question before taking a drag on his Columbian from Old City Coffee. I sipped my Balzac and nodded.

"Like a charm," I answered as the app zoomed in once more to show me the layout of the interior of the building. "Told you this works. It's awesome. Gabby rocks!" I was a little giddy.

"Yea, still getting a signal with that tucked into her panties. Amazing," Linc remarked. He was clearly less impressed than I. The app zoomed one more time into the lower level before picking up the moving green dot.

"I love technology!" Linc just shook his head at me and took another sip of his coffee. We sat there for a solid five minutes watching the green dot move to and fro inside the club. Every so often someone would come up to the door, look at the camera and gain entrance to the building.

"Lowlifes…" Linc muttered after a guy pulled up in a Mercedes and went inside.

When the last bit of sunlight was finally gone, Linc and I sprung into action. We were alongside the building in a moment. Remembering that the door locks automatically we waited around the corner for someone to arrive. A dark blue Jaguar XJ12 rolled into the lot and I saw our opportunity coming. The man stood a tad over six feet and was wearing a cleanly pressed blue suit with a blue and yellow striped tie. He could have just stepped out of the courtroom. Mr. Blue stood in front of the door, looked up and then pulled the door open. Like a slightly chubby house cat, I rolled to the door just as Linc put a bullet in the camera. My foot slid in the doorjamb just in time to keep it from closing.

"Bingo!" I exclaimed, but the sound of the camera going to pieces caught Mr. Blue's attention.

"Hey you, who do you think you are! I'm calling security." He turned but before he could utter another sound Linc Diesel had swept past me, through the door and had one hand around the suit's mouth and the other with his .38 snub nose pressed firmly to suit's head.

"You've got a choice here. You can shut up, get in your car and get the hell out of here or you can yell and see what I might do to you." Linc increased the pressure on the man's mouth, gritted his teeth and continued, "Your choice, dough boy. I'm going to count to three; when I do, I'd highly recommend you scream for security because I want to carve you up like a jack-o-lantern. One…. Two… Three…" And Linc let him go. The man didn't even look back. He ran so fast through the door he almost leveled me on the way back to his Jaguar. The car tore out of the lot at such a high velocity I'm not even sure he had time to consider which way he was going.

"Lowlife…" Linc muttered before turning his attention to the door on the other side of the warehouse with lights and music coming from behind it. "We'd better move. It won't take them long to come and investigate that camera being out." He started to walk toward the door with his .38 in his hand.

"Hey, yo… Linc, you're gonna want to holster that."

Philadelphia Story by Bruce A. Sarte

I ran after him and was about to grab his shoulder when he spun back toward me.

"Good idea." And he made the gun disappear. I looked at him again and then approached the door. We both stopped and I pulled out my phone again. I located the green circle that represented Jenny and nodded my head.

"OK, looks like she's in one of the back rooms. Same place she was a few minutes ago before we came in so she's either with a john or maybe she's got our buddy Ming in a corner. Best thing to do here is to just look like you belong... Hey, Linc!" He had already opened the door and walked into the club. "Dammit, Linc!"

The moment I crossed over the threshold and back into the club the lights hit me and the music enveloped me. The uniquely sharp vocals of Tony Lewis from *Main Attraction* by The Outfield was cutting through my head.

I'd like to see if you're for real,
So can't we make some kind of deal, yea
You say there's no such word as can't
Making you the girl that I want

A kaleidoscope of colored lights kept hitting my eyes and I couldn't keep track of where Linc was. I kept scanning from the stage to the bar and trying to see into the crowd of overdressed old men and underdressed young women. The club area was nothing like I remembered it, they must have remodeled in the very short time since I'd last been here. There was a young, thin blonde with only her black panties and bra on slithering up and down the stage. The stage was in the same place as before but it looked like they added an additional pole and better lighting. The reds and blues hit the girl, making her look almost alien as she arched her back and spun on her ass with her legs akimbo. I tilted my head to get a better angle on the exact curvature of her hind quarters when a strong hand gripped my shoulder.

"This way compadre." Linc darted from behind me and headed over to where the *rooms* were. Before I could respond he was already halfway there. I pulled my phone out and checked the app—there was the green dot dead ahead. Linc was almost at the entrance to the rooms when my old friend Maurice stepped in front of him and said something to him. I didn't hear what Maurice said to Linc, but as suddenly as he stepped in front of him, his facial expression changed from the big tough guy to the pained little boy. And then Maurice fell to the ground. I picked up the pace and caught up to shadow Linc as he entered the hallway that led to the rooms.

"You got her?" he barked over his shoulder.

"Got her, third room on the left," I answered as we approached the pulled curtain. We locked eyes.

"One..."

"Two," I responded, and then in unison: "Three!" We yelled as we threw the curtain open with guns drawn and pointed directly at the naked back of a young topless woman grinding on the lap of a faceless middle aged man.

"Jenny, get down!" I yelled. She spun and covered her breasts with a shocked look on her face, revealing a salt-and-peppered haired man. He snapped his head forward, cheeks flush with passion and fear in his eyes.

"What the fuck is going on?!" he yelled, throwing Jennifer off his lap onto the floor as he bolted upright.

"Uncle Lance, what are you doing!" She grabbed at her top and turned away. I turned back to the old dude who stood with his boner pushing the limits of his trousers. He stood way too close for my personal comfort.

"Sir, sit the fuck down," I commanded, and the cool thing about having a gun, he listened.

"Jennifer," Linc began, "this isn't Mister M, is it?"

"Mister who?" Salt-and-pepper demanded.

"Shut up!" all three of us yelled at the same time.

"You guys have to get out of here! NOW!" Jennifer wailed pointing our way out.

"Where is M?" I demanded.

"He's not here tonight!" she answered through gritted teeth, "Now go before Wade or Maurice come and beat my ass for this!"

"I don't think Maurice is going to be a problem." Linc started matter-of-factly, got up and left the room. I shook my head and put Betsy away.

"Dammit."

Chapter Twelve

At five minutes past three in the morning, Jennifer emerged from front door of the #1 Velvet Dragon. She looked our way but turned to the right and began walking across the parking lot. When she disappeared on the other side of the fence I fired up the Camaro and slowly pulled around the other side of the fence alongside her.

"Come on," I yelled out the window, "hop in." She jumped in the back of the car and we sped off into the city.

"I'm sorry, Lance, really I am. He wasn't there... I had no way to tell you," she said from the back seat. Her voice was tight and pleading with me to understand.

"Yea, what the hell... of all nights, tonight Ming picks to not show up."

"He wasn't here tonight but I think I know why. I heard the other girls talking. They were talking about Linda, how she hadn't been in to work lately. I think it has something to do with her. Mister M had to do something with her."

"Linda?" I said with some interest. "What kind of something?"

"I don't know, really. Just something..."

"Let it go, cowboy," Linc said simply. He knew what I was thinking and for the duration of our ride back to the

Ben Franklin I sat silently mulling over my options. It was almost four in the morning when I pulled the Camaro up to the Chestnut Street entrance to the Ben.

"Here guys, hop out and go on up," I said, flipping my access card to Linc. "I'll park and head up shortly." I motioned my head toward the parking garage. Linc looked at me long and hard for about ten seconds.

"You sure, cowboy?" Linc asked, looking through the open passenger window.

I nodded. "Yea, I'm sure. See you in a bit." I stomped on the accelerator and sped off down Chestnut, not even pretending to go to the parking garage. I whipped the car around the corner of 6th and Chestnut, speeding toward Vine to get to the Packard as fast as I could. I pulled the car around the back of the Packard near the service entrance. Checking my iPhone saw that it was about four thirty. I pulled the car into a spot behind a truck parked behind a dumpster. About fifteen minutes later a delivery truck from one of the food vendors pulled up behind the building and I saw my opportunity. I slipped out of the car and hid behind the parked truck waiting for the delivery doors to open. It was amazing how quiet the city could be at a few minutes before five. I could actually hear movement inside the loading dock and a minute later the garage-style door flew up and a guy in a blue jumpsuit came out to greet the truck driver. After a brief exchange the guy in the jumpsuit told the driver to follow him into the loading dock. Once they were out of sight, I carefully made my way into the loading dock area behind some stacked crates. The large open space served as storage for the banquet hall and conference center in the basement of the old building. Looking around, this back area looked every bit its age and seemed to have an individual smell for every year it had stood. I wiped my nose to try and remove the stench but it did no good. The noise from the idling truck ten feet away was loud in here but I could hear the two guys talking just a few feet on the other side of the crates. After a quick survey of the area I saw a closed door on the other side of the room. Since this seemed like my best option I darted off toward the door with no regard for being seen. I was through the door before anyone noticed, or at least I don't think anyone noticed. The hallway had a dulled laminate yellow floor - or maybe it used to be white? The walls were painted a dingy grey color and had black marks all over them from where trays, carts and other things being brought from the loading dock had marked their appearance. After a minute of walking, I made a right turn down an adjoining hallway. I looked all around me but with no new information, I had to keep going. I walked another twenty feet until I came upon what I was looking for: The Service Elevator.

"Shazam!" I exclaimed and was even more pleasantly surprised that it was sitting open and waiting. "For me? Don't mind if I do," I remarked as I stepped onto the elevator, pulled the gate shut and pressed the round, black number eight. The elevator jumped to life, slowly pulling me toward the eighth floor. Each floor that the elevator passed made a sickly dinging sound and after the eighth sound of pain the elevator moaned to a halt. I stood for a moment listening for sounds outside the elevator, satisfied there were none, as carefully as I could, I pulled the gate from its locking point and poked my head out into the dimly lit hallway. A quick glance told me the access to the main hallway was off to the left, so I hopped out of the elevator and was upon the door in a moment. Taking a deep breath I pushed the door open as casually as I could and entered the hallway. I began walking as nonchalantly as possible looking at each door as I passed.

"Eight twenty… eight sixteen… eight fourteen…" I rounded the corner and found what I came for. "Eight ten and not good…" There was a sight I never liked to see. The door slightly ajar and the doorframe cracked. "Looks like forced entry to me…" I mumbled as I pulled Betsy from her holster and slowly pushed the door open the rest of the way.

"Hellllooooo…." I announced loud enough for anyone to hear, but not so loud to be alarming. "Just me, your neighborhood detective man." I peered into the kitchen and saw a sink full of dishes and the door to the microwave open. Continuing into the living room I saw signs of a struggle. Pillows from the sofa were all over the floor and an end table was turned on its side, the associated lamp lay in pieces next to it. After quickly clearing the smaller bedroom I found myself standing in the middle of a war zone, otherwise referred to as the master bedroom. What was previously well put together and an attractive space was ransacked and broken. The mirror was smashed, lamps were broken and the bed looked like someone had used it for quite the sexual escapade… but I somehow doubted that is what happened here. I flipped the light switch on the wall illuminating the scene with the overhead light and to my horror found blood stains in several places on the bed. A glint of metal caught my eye on the floor. I bent over and found a gold necklace. When I picked it up I found a heart shaped pendant dangling from it. It was one of those that opened and contained a picture inside. Before I flipped it open, I knew whose necklace this was. Opening it to reveal a picture of the little boy only confirmed it. Something had happened to Linda. I reached into my pocket to pull my phone out, but then I heard people in the hallway outside the apartment.

"Hello, Philadelphia Police. We are entering the dwelling. Is there anyone here?" I quickly put Betsy in her holster and rubbed my face in frustration.

"Shit…" I muttered before answering. "Yes, in the master bedroom. I'm a private detective working on a case and I am armed."

"Sir, stay where you are," The officer commanded from the other room and I did as he asked knowing that my window of opportunity had now closed.

* * *

"For the third time, I am a private detective… you have my creds. I was there looking for Linda Sanders or Linda Sanderson, I'm not sure what her real name is. She hired me to find her son."

"The one who isn't missing?" the baby faced detective sarcastic asked for the third time.

"Yes, I think… I don't really know." The light from above was disconcerting but it beat the pants off the two-way glass behind Detective Babypants.

"You don't really know?" He leaned back in his chair. "You aren't much of a detective, now are you?" I inhaled deeply, partially to center myself before giving my answer and partially to center myself and prevent me from launching my body over the table at him. That wouldn't end well for either of us.

"It is complicated and, quite frankly, none of your business, Casper Babypants." He didn't like that.

"Actually it is, smartass. I've got you on breaking and entering, trespassing and a person of interest in a possible missing persons case. The blood on the bed has your name written all over it, Carter. All over it!" He repeated for emphasis.

"You've got nothing, you can't even hold me. B&E? Really? Says who? I entered the building, found the door already open and was investigating. Case closed, now either charge me or let me go. Now. Before I lawyer up."

"Lawyer?" He laughed and got up to leave the room. "I guess we're done here. We'll be holding you for the full twenty-four hours then... if we can't hold you on the B&E, I guess we'll let you go. Good luck finding your car..." He reached for the door handle and began turning it.

"Where's Phishkit? I think you need to go get Lieutenant Phishkit now and ask him what you should do with me. That might educate your punk ass a little."

"Phishkit?" His demeanor changed completely, he was no longer so sure of himself and he reached up and loosened his dirty white collar just a bit. "Why would Lieutenant Phishkit give a rat's ass about you?" His words were tough but the tone of his voice did not convey the feigned attitude. In answer to his query, I unbuttoned the sleeve on my shirt and rolled it up to reveal a tattoo on my right forearm. The tattoo was of a seal, holding a harpoon and sporting a bad attitude.

"Why don't you ask him about *his* tattoo?"

It took about fifteen minutes before a uniformed officer was escorting me down the hall from the perp area to the conference room. It may have been for families and officers, but it really wasn't much nicer than the interrogation rooms. The real upside was it was brighter and there was a pitcher of water on the table. I poured myself a paper cup full and drank it down. I hadn't realized how thirsty I was until maybe my fourth full paper cup.

"You!" Phishkit jammed his head into the room

through the door. "Don't move!" he barked at me. I nodded, mouth full of water and he disappeared the same way he came in. Three cups of water later he re-entered the room with a folder in one hand and the other running through his hair.

"Alright," he seemed to be talking to himself, "how do you know Linda Sanderson?"

"She's a client. Hired me to find her son. I'm…"

"The one who isn't actually missing?" He interrupted, "Yea, Johnson briefed me on that."

"Yea, right… I think it was all a hoax. Something to distract me from something else.. maybe scare me away, I don't know exactly."

"And you were at her apartment because…"

"It's a long story, but the short of it was I was looking for Linda. I thought she might be in danger."

"Danger?" This made his eyebrows tent up. "What made you think she'd be in danger?" He pulled out a chair on the other side of the table and sat.

"This other case I have… I didn't realize it until today but they are related. I uncovered something that made me concerned for Linda's safety and pretty much confirmed that Linda's case was bogus."

"*What*," he looked pointedly at me, "did you uncover, Lance?"

"Come on, Foster, you know I can't tell you that. It's privileged information that relates to a different case." He shut his eyes tightly before sliding the folder in my direction. I looked at it, afraid to touch it as if it were contaminated in some way.

"What is this?" I asked, not really wanting the answer.

"Open it, flat-foot. Then let's see how much water

that client bullshit holds." He looked angry. So I opened the folder to reveal pictures of a battered and bloody Linda Sanderson. She had been badly beaten and had her throat slashed.

"Oh, Linda..." I muttered under my breath. I flipped from picture to picture taking in the sheer brutality of the scenes.

"Now... you were saying about how you knew? Because if I'm being objective about the whole thing, you're our prime suspect, Carter." My head jerked up in response to that.

"I was..." And I thought about where I was before I finished that answer. "When did you find her?"

"About a half an hour ago, that's one of the locked storage areas by the river. ME puts the time of death around midnight... where were you at midnight, Carter?"

"I have witnesses, I was with people," I said matter-of-factly and considering how much to actually let Phishkit in on this. "Ram Don Ming."

"Are you telling me that Ram Don Ming, the Asian crime boss is your alibi?" Shock crossed his features like a dancer across a stage; there... and then gone.

"No! No wonder you never went into private detecting. You're thick. Ming killed Linda Sanderson. Where's her boy? Do you know anything about the boy?"

He nodded. "The boy is safe with his grandparents in Lancaster. They said he's been down on the farm there for about a week." That made me nod.

"See, the whole thing was a hoax." I stood and started pacing. "I need time, Pussycat." I eased back into our familiar pattern of discourse.

"Time? I can't give you time. I have to find a killer and you're pointing your finger at someone who is virtually untouchable. Hello? Carter? Anyone home?" He faked knocking on his head to illustrate his point.

"Yea, yea... I get that. But my other case... it's all related. I've given you a lead... Ram Don Ming... he's got some goons that do his dirty work. One guy has tattoos all down his arms, you know, like sleeves? And the other one has a crucifix right here." And I pointed. "You can find them at the warehouse for Sparkle Industries. Here." I wrote down the address. "That's where... that's all I have for you right now. I need more time to put the rest of my case together, then..." I nodded, "then Ming will go down."

Phishkit sat back in his chair and considered what I had just told him and started shaking his head. "That's not enough, flat-foot."

"Here, see this." I pulled my shirt up to reveal bruising and pointed to the lesions on my head. "They did this to me. Sleeves and Crucifix—I'm filing formal charges. That should be enough to pick them up and hold them. Right?"

The head shaking continued but his answer was different. "Alright, you fill out the paperwork and we'll go get them. You know that's not going to hold them for long right? And that's still not Ming."

"I know, but you give me twenty-four hours and I promise you Ming will never be a problem for you again."

I filled out the paperwork. Sleeves and Crucifix were now wanted men, for all the good it would do.

Chapter Thirteen

It wasn't until I was on the elevator going up to my apartment that the weight of what I had just promised Phishkit hit me. I approached my door shaking my head and realized I didn't have my access card.

"Crap." I looked at my door and hoped *someone* was there. *Knock, knock.* I heard paws flittering on the other side of the door as Copper sniffed at the bottom. "Hey buddy, anyone home?" The answer came when he door flew open and there stood the beautiful frame of Nathalie.

"Hey, stranger. Where you been? I heard you went on a hunting trip?" I smiled and reached out to take her into a long embrace.

"You have no idea." She slid her arms around my waist to return the hug.

"So," she said, breaking the embrace and walking toward the kitchen. "What's been going on since you ran out on me? I met your friends. I mean, Linc was here with some girl when I came up to check on you."

"Linc? Where'd he go? Did he take her with him?" I asked with maybe too much emphasis on the words.

"Yea," she answered with concern in her voice. "Why? Who was she? I tried to talk to Linc but, well you know him... he had nothing to say. He just gave me your access card and left with the girl."

I nodded my head and pulled out my phone. I started typing out a text message to Linc when Nathalie caught my attention.

"Lance, *who was the girl?*" She was in front of me now, and I hadn't even notice her cross the room again as I tapped out my message.

Linc, where you at? Is J with you?

"She's just…" I stammered looking for the right words. "She's a client is all. I ran into some trouble, got hung up at the police station for a while." I looked at the time and it was almost dinner time. "A long while. Man, am I starving." I tried my best to change the subject. "What's cooking, hot stuff?" I walked into the kitchen to smell what was on the stove but Nathalie grabbed my arm.

"A client? She was awfully pretty." She pulled me close again and slid her soft hands under my shirt. "Do I have something to worry about, Mister Private Detective?" She smiled as she started kissing my neck and running her fingers south of the border. As hungry and concerned about Jennifer as I was, my libido began to betray me and I think Nathalie noticed. She took in a breath as she pushed her hips into mine and nibbled on my ear at the same time. My hands began to find their way down her back to the gentle curves of her backside. Just as my fingers began to get creative around the valley of her cheeks, my phone dinged twice, signaling a reply from Linc. Nathalie pulled away slightly.

"Maybe after dinner we can…" she smiled and licked her lips heavily, "see where this all goes." She lazily pulled her arm from me and went back to whatever was on the stove. Shaking my head, I said nothing and looked at my phone.

Office. Yes. You OK?

I tapped out my reply quickly.

Yes, meet you later.

Nathalie had prepared a wonderful dinner of chicken cacciatore with linguine and a loaf of fresh Italian bread complete with a bottle of Cabernet Sauvignon. We ate and didn't really say much until the bottle of wine was gone. I watched the candle light dance in the glass as Nathalie took the last sip of her wine. A small drip escaped her mouth, she quickly lapped it with her tongue.

"So..." she slurred just slightly and stood up, "how you feeling over there?"

"Me?" I answered coyly, playing along a little.

She stepped over to me and pulled my chair out. "Is this more comfortable?" She asked as she straddled me and pushed her weight down on my lap. Looking up into those glassy emerald eyes put me into a trance that encompassed my head and removed everything else from my mind. When her soft ruby lips met mine I felt electricity pass between us. It was as if she had a desire that was stored up within her that she transferred into me through her soft and passionate kiss. My body responded. She started to move her hips slowly on top of mine, working my passion up to meet hers. I ran my hands up her back, slyly pushing her top off over her head in one motion breaking our kiss for just a moment. Her breathy kiss returned to my lips at the same time my fingers deftly undid the clap on the back of her bra letting her soft milky breasts fall free.

"It's been a long time, you know..." I admitted, breaking our kiss.

She reached down inside the front of my pants. "No way to tell from here...." She rejoined our lips with a new, more vibrant passion and I responded. I stood, her legs wrapped around my waist and moved into the bedroom to finish our dessert.

* * *

After our lovemaking we fell fast asleep in each other's arms. I awoke several hours later to the sound of *Hell's Bells* coming from the kitchen. I looked down at Nathalie's love-tousled hair and slowly eased my way out of her embrace. I didn't make it to the phone in time, and Linc left a voicemail.

"Where are you?" His tone even and matter-of-fact in spite of him asking a question. "Jennifer went to work. She's not back yet. I don't know where she is. Call me." I looked at the time and saw it was a little after two in the morning. I hit the contact entry for Linc. It rang only once and he greeted me with, "I'm coming to you. Stay there."

"How long?" I asked pensively.

"Too long." And I knew he was right.

"I'll meet you in the lobby in five." I hung up without waiting for a response. I already knew what his response would be. I threw on some jeans and a button down flannel. Copper stared at me as I strapped Betsy on, he cocked his head slightly as if to ask *Where ya off to, buddy?*

"I think Jenny's in trouble, furry compadre." I reached down and rubbed his chin. He responded with a quick lick on the top of my hand and trotted off into the living room. He hopped on the couch, circled and rested with his head looking at the door. Copper's concern made me concerned. Did he know something I didn't? I went to reach for my brown leather jacket, but a hand took hold of my wrist.

"Lance?" Her voice was soft and worried. "Where are you going at this time of night?"

"Someone's in trouble, I have to…"

"Who?" Then I saw her face darken. "It's that girl, the pretty one, isn't it?" she said accusingly.

"Nat, she's a client." I lied a little. "She's missing, I have to find her."

"How can she be missing. She was *just here!*" She actually seemed a little angry.

"Whoa!" I put my hands up in defense. "Go back to bed. I'll be back in no time." I kissed her forehead and pushed past her to the door.

"Don't you dare kiss my forehead like I'm your lap dog now that I've slept with you. That… that girl is nothing but trouble. I can tell trouble when I see it." She pointed at her chest for emphasis. She was wearing my bathrobe. It looked good.

"Listen, Jenny needs my help. Some bad guys are following her and trying to hurt her. Linc and I are all she's got." I slammed the door behind me and headed down to the lobby. I got to the 8th Street entrance at about the same time that Linc was pulling up in his vintage 1967 Corvette Coupe that he had repainted the original yellow color. It was a stunning vehicle to see and a whale of a good time to drive.

"Nathalie there?"

I looked at him as the car roared towards Market Street. "Yea, how'd you know."

He looked over at me and frowned, just a tad. "It's all over your face, cowboy. Hope you enjoyed the ride. I think we're in for a long night."

"To the Moshulu?" He nodded and turned right onto Market toward the river. Linc weaved in and out of traffic. It is surprising how many people are out on Market Street at almost three in the morning. The engine roared and the street lights flew by until we hit the Head House Square district near Old City. The lights drifted into the background as we zipped through the quiet neighborhood at high speed. Linc slammed on the brakes and did a *Starsky & Hutch*-esque turn with the tail of the car coming almost all the way around before he slammed the car into second gear and brought the engine back to life roaring towards the boat.

"She said she was going to go get some stuff after work. Then come back. Thought it was a good idea for her to go to work. Not piss off Ming."

I nodded in agreement but could feel the anxiety welling up inside me. "No word from her?"

"None." The rest of the ride down Columbus was in silence. We pulled into the parking lot to find a black BMW 735i parked blocking the gangway to the boat. Linc pulled the Vette in front of the BMW, blocking its path forward.

"They could still back up…" I said as he got out of the car. In response, Linc pulled a hunting knife from him jacket and proceeds to put it three inches deep into the drivers side front tire. With a loud *pop* followed by a soft *whoosh,* Linc demolished each tire making sure to turn the knife up and slice the sidewall into several pieces on the way out.

"You were saying?" He walked up the gangway, which was not chained tonight. I nodded and followed without a word. That Linc, he knows how to make his presence known. I was two steps up the gangway when I heard a thumping sound coming from the trunk of the BMW.

"Linc, wait!" I shouted and ran to the trunk. "Hello?" I yelled at the trunk. I got a muffled scream and some more thumping. As quickly as I could I was at the driver's door and pulling at the handle but the door was locked. I pulled Betsy out, stepped back and fired a shot at the window shattering it into a million small shards of glass. Reaching in, I pulled the handle releasing the lock mechanism and opening the door. I searched the dash until I finally found the automatic trunk release.

"You need to hurry. We've attracted some unwelcome attention!" Linc yelled as he fired a shot off in the boat's direction. There were a couple of other gun shots but either these guys were terrible shots or they were shooting at us. I pushed the release to open the trunk and heard the pop of the latch.

"Got it!" I announced triumphantly before I realized what they were shooting at. Linc let a couple more shots go and I saw a spark flash off the trunk lid of the car. "Shit!" I yelled. I fired back at the deck of the boat, unsure who or what I was actually shooting at. "Cover me!" I was ducked behind the back of the car before any more shots could be fired.

"Uncle Lance!" Jenny screamed as scared as I've ever heard anyone. Two more shots rang out and ricocheted off the asphalt near my feet.

"Here," I offered my hand up, "grab my hand. I'll pull you out. Stay low!" She did as I asked and ended up face-first onto the parking lot. "Sorry. I did the best I could." She nodded at me in acknowledgment. Linc fired off another shot.

"Thank God…" Jenny said almost to herself. "They were going to… they said they were going to cut me open!" She hugged herself to me as a shot blew out the back driver's side window. I reached into my jacket and pulled out a knife. I quickly cut her hands loose, she rubbed at her wrists. They were red and looked raw.

"Go," I pointed around the car, "get in the passenger's side of Linc's car." She nodded and looked around the corner. "Stay low and out of sight. They seem to be focused here, I'll keep the focus here." I stood and fired two shots at the unseen gunmen.

"Got it. I can do this," she reaffirmed herself and slinked around the corner as Linc fired two shots.

"Linc," I stood and fired a round, "get in the car, get out of here. She is in it." There was no response from Linc. He fired a shot at the boat, I heard a scream and a splash. "Nice shooting, Tex." I looked over — Linc was gone and his car was roaring off out of the parking lot. The gunmen fired at his car repeatedly. I took two more shots, when it was obvious they didn't care I ran down to the bow of the boat and started firing at the bottom of the car. One... two... three... down to only two more rounds... four... and BOOM. The car went up like a Roman candle at an Independence Day celebration. As the car erupted I saw the yellow Corvette rolling towards safety. I decided this would be the perfect diversion to use to make my exit, and so I did. I made tracks running as fast as my aching feet would take me toward the boulevard, I turned to look over my shoulder to look at the now destroyed luxury car. The flames reached upward as if they were grasping at sky and failing each time. My pace slowed, I turned my eyes back toward the road only to be met by three large men standing ten feet in front of me. I tripped over myself trying to stop from running into them, landing hard on my hands and knees.

"Oh, damn..." I held picked my hands up to removed the gravel from my palms.

"Mister Carter," began one of the men. I didn't look up to see which one before something connected heavily with the top of my head and I went down like a sack of potatoes. My face was stinging as something kept hitting it over and over. It brought me back to reality, if nothing else.

"What the hell?" I brought my hands up to shield my face.

"As I was saying before you so rudely passed out..." A man with a faint Asian accent. Was that Korean? Maybe Chinese? "I bring a message for you from our most honorable master."

"Your most honorable what?" I managed to get out before a foot met my left side. How very terrible to meet you, Mister Foot.

"Our most honorable master must insist that you deliver the technology to us at once. If you do not, we will be forced to simply take it and that would not be pretty for any of you. Especially your precious Jennifer."

"The what?"

"Are we clear, Mister Carter?"

"I have no idea what the hell..." The largest of the three black-clad men grabbed me by the front of my shirt and hauled me to my feet in one swoop of his enormous arms. The one who was speaking was only slightly smaller than the one who was man-handling me.

"Deliver the technology, Mister Carter. Find it, bring it to us. This is not a request and the master will not give you another chance."

I stood dumbfounded as the three men pushed past me and walked toward the burning car. I could hear sirens blaring off in the distance, which meant the authorities, were on their way. There was no way I wanted to be anywhere near this place when they arrived. A little more battered and bruised than before, I began my trek across the footbridge that connected South Street with the riverfront and made my way home on foot.

Chapter Fourteen

"I never saw them coming... I swear. They were like ghosts. I was walking to my train and then some dude had me over his shoulder some other dude put tape on my mouth." Jennifer's head was shaking, her hands were fumbling with her necklace and the tears started coming again. "I never saw them..." Nathalie reached out and put her arm around Jennifer trying to comfort her.

"It's alright..." she kept saying quietly, adding "Monsters... they are just monsters."

"They want that information, Jenny," I said, pacing the living room floor. The sun was cutting in through the window casting a rectangular brightness on my carpet. Copper came into the room and decided to make use of this opportunity to work on his tan. "I know this is going to be hard," I continued, sitting on the end of the coffee table across fro Jennifer. "Is there anything... anything at all you can think of that seems... I don't know..." I fumbled around the words. "Out of the ordinary or strange that happened around the time your mom died?"

"Died?" she choked out. "Uncle Lance, you were there. They cut her up! They mutilated her, Uncle Lance!" she shouted at me. I nodded my head and put my hand on her bare knee to try and calm her. I looked at Nathalie who was giving me a dirty look and then back to Jenny, still dressed from work in a skin tight black leather mini-skirt and now-dirty white sweater that hugged her breasts and showed plenty of cleavage.

"I'm sorry, Jenny, but I need you to think… think about things your mother did. Something that might seem odd or out of place."

"That was ten years ago… I was just a kid." She was shaking her head but her eyes were darting back and forth considering something.

"Your mom was a waitress," I said, trying to help her along. "You used to spend time with your grandmother while your mom would work shifts, right?"

"Yea," she said. "You know it is." Her answer sounded standoffish but her eyes were still working.

"Did your mom have any boyfriends?"

Her eyes stopped and stared at me. "Boyfriends?" Her eyes narrowed and seared my forehead with an intensity I'd not seen from her before. "*You,*" she said accusingly, "were her boyfriend. She wasn't like that. Don't you know? She wasn't a…" Her words trailed off and she broke the stare. "…whore like me."

"Hey." I took her hands in mine and leaned forward to try and get her gaze back. I continued in a softer tone, "You are not a whore, Jennifer. You are in a bad spot right now but we are going to fix it… we are. I promise you that." There I go, promising everything and having nothing to give. "Your mom, she was a great lady. I cared for her very, very deeply but I wasn't her boyfriend."

She looked a little confused and maybe even a bit betrayed. "What?"

"No." I shook my head. "Your mom was someone who was there for me when…" Carolyn's face raced through my mind. "During one of the most difficult times in my life."

"What," she stopped, "happened?"

"Twelve years ago, I was in love. I had someone" I looked at Nathalie who seemed to be listening to everything intently, "who was very close to me. We shared everything... good, bad and in the middle... or at least I thought we did. I found out she was mixed up in something," I paused and drew in a breath, "awful. And being the guy I am, I couldn't stay out of the middle of it. I tried to get her out... I tried... then one night I went to her apartment to pick her up and found her there." The image of Carolyn sprawled out on the couch with cocaine spilled over her coffee table, a needle on the floor and her eyes staring vacantly off into nothing. There was blood around her eyes. I'll remember that forever. "She had overdosed and I didn't even know she was doing drugs. I was so blind to it all."

"Overdose?" Jennifer mouthed to herself. Nathalie looked confused.

"She OD'ed?" Nathalie asked. I answered with a nod.

"I'm so sorry, Lance." Jennifer said.

"The point is that your mom was her best friend. We both didn't understand what had happened. We didn't understand how she overdosed... but at least we didn't understand together." Jennifer nodded her head in understanding.

"I just don't remember... I remember you. I remember my grandmother and going to school. But I just can't remember anything specific. I remember this." She offered up the key necklace and seemed frustrated.

"What is that?"

"A necklace my mom gave me... right after my surgery. She said it would open a great door for me one day." She laughed quietly. "It's all I have left of her."

"It's beautiful." Nathalie said softly.

"No new people around that time? Do you remember her ever making you go to your room when someone came over or something like that?" I went back to forty questions.

"No, no no!" She was insistent, the frustration returned. "I can't remember!"

"I used to come over twice a week, to your apartment on 3rd. Do you remember that?"

She nodded. "I remember you coming over but not how often. It just seemed like you always came over, ya know?" I nodded.

"Did she give you anything — anything to hide?" Nathalie interjected. We both looked at her like she had two-heads. "What? I'm just trying to help."

"Yea," I said and went back to Jennifer, "and we'd go out to dinner? At the diner?"

"I remember." She smiled. "You'd always make me eat apple pie. I'd tell you I didn't like it but I did. I loved apple pie."

"I know." I smiled back. "Do you remember there was a time that you and your mom went away? You went somewhere and came back?"

"Went away?" She looked at me.

"Yea, you missed a weeks' worth of dinner with me, but your mom told me she couldn't tell me why. I don't recall much more of that." Jennifer looked like she was thinking deeply. "Oh, that was right before the operation."

"Right," I answered, "you had to have your kidney removed. It was an emergency. Your mom just called me out of the blue to tell me she wouldn't be around because you had the surgery. I never did get to see you in the hospital. Every time I asked where you were she'd have to get off the phone."

"I don't remember much from the whole thing, just the stupid scar I have." She looked at Nathalie. "I'm sure you know all about that being a doctor and all."

"Oh," Nathalie responded, "I'm not quite a doctor yet."

"Thankfully, it is at least where no one can see it," she smiled slightly, "if it were up higher than my skirt, Mr. M probably wouldn't let me dance. Who knows what he'd have me doing."

Nathalie looked confused. "What do you mean? Where is it?"

"You know," Jennifer rolled onto her side and pulled up the side of her skirt to reveal what looked like a postage stamp size scar on her hip. I looked at it.

"That's from your kidney?" I asked.

"Yea, I don't remember much about it but that's what Mom said." Nathalie looked at me, then got up and quickly walked into the kitchen. "I do remember Mom was on the phone a lot, you know, while I was in bed and on the couch recovering for that week or two."

"Do you have any clue who she might have been talking to?"

"No, I'm pretty sure I was on some kind of pain meds." I nodded in agreement.

"OK, back to last night. Did the guys who took you say anything in particular?"

She instinctively began rubbing at her wrists. They were still red—they would bruise up soon. "They kept asking for the information, the..."

"Technology?" I prompted.

"Yes!" she responded. "How did you know that?"

"I had a little encounter myself, but you go on."

"They kept asking for the information and big guy kept saying that I'd," she did her impression of the big guy, *"better hand over the technology or they would cut me up."* She went back to her normal voice. "It was very scary. The big guy went left me tied up in this room for a few minutes and then other guys came back, threw me in the trunk of that car and drove off. I really thought I was going to die. When they put me in the trunk, I thought it was over..." She began to sob quietly. "Then you showed up... again to save me." She put her head down on my knee and began to cry softly.

"OK, alright." I ran my hand through her hair. "You're going to stay here, with me. We will watch you twenty-four hours. You'll be safe." I heard my front door click as I finished the sentence. Apparently Nathalie didn't like that plan.

Chapter Fifteen

The morning turned into afternoon and while Jennifer slept on the couch I pulled out my MacBook to do some research. I pulled up the death records database and started doing some crosschecking of dates. I typed in *Lindsey Collins* to pull up her death record. I stared at the date and cause of death.

Gun shot wound to the head.

I flashed back to that night... that phone call... the drive. I remembered the rain. I remembered the pain created by the intense feeling of helplessness.

"...*there's nothing you can do for me – they are coming to get me!*"

I clenched my fists and squeezed my eyes shut. The images of Lindsey sprawled across her living room floor came at me like 3D stereoscopic images through a viewfinder. The image of blood splattered all over her couch. That indicating someone stood over her and pulled the trigger. But not before they had cut her. They took a knife to the sides of her face, then her ribs and stomach and arms. The sick fucks tortured her before, finally and mercifully, they killed her. I shook my head to clear that imagery out from the deepest recesses of my mind. I opened a new browser window and typed in the URL for the detective background check website. Once logged in, I typed *Jennifer Collins* and watched a nifty little spyglass icon dance back and forth across the screen. While I was waiting for that to come back, I opened another browser window and typed in *Lindsey Collins*. The resulting dancing spyglass caused me to click back over to Jennifer's background check. It brought up a picture of Jennifer that was a police-booking photo from two years ago. She'd gotten arrested for soliciting at eighteen. I shook my head, but hit print on the picture anyway. Scrolling through the rest of the report I made note of a few interesting items. The date she was placed into the child services database, the name of her first foster family and the date she was placed with them. I stopped copying and pasting once I noticed a pattern. She was in and out of nine foster homes in six years and then she was placed in the tenth home. I looked at the exit date and it was listed as UNKNOWN. She'd run away. I looked over at the couch and felt an intense sense of failure and shame. I felt like I could have… I should have done something. Looking back to the screen I clicked on the browser window that was running the report on Lindsey Collins. Except when I scrolled down I saw the words:

FILE LOCKED

I tried it again. After a few minutes the same message appeared. I didn't understand. I pulled up Apple Mail and shot off a quick e-mail to Gabby asking her to check and make sure my account was set up correctly. To see if I was locked out of something that I need access to and to make it happen in her best techie kind of way. Next it was time to give Rhonda another call. I picked up my iPhone and was looking for her contact when there were two knocks on the door. It was Linc, he'd come back to check on Jennifer.

"What's the plan, cowboy?" His words said one thing but his casual gaze to the couch told me otherwise. The plan was secondary: just like me, he wanted to ensure Jennifer's safety.

"Someone needs to be with her twenty-four-seven. Never alone."

He nodded. "She going back?"

"No, they were going to throw her in the river. I'm sure of it," I answered matter-of-factly. "But I need to run down some leads... mine some information. Can you hang here for a couple of clicks? Let me check a few rabbit holes?" I looked at the couch where Jennifer slept quietly and then back to Linc. He nodded and went into the kitchen.

"Going to eat," he said. I picked up my keys and headed out the door. By the time I'd reached my car I had Rhonda on the phone.

"You want what?" she screeched through the phone.

"Lindsey Collins, 215-555-2711. I need her phone records from ten years ago — an entire year's worth if possible. Can you do it?"

"Dinner," she said simply as I pulled out of the parking garage and headed off toward The Moshulu.

"Dinner?" I was caught a little off-guard.

"Yes, dinner. I get you what you need, you take me to dinner. And I mean a nice dinner, Lancey, not Gino's!" I could hear her chewing her gum intensely on the other end of the phone while I considered her offer. I sat idling within view of Independence Hall when my call waiting beeped in my ear. I pulled the phone away to see the smiling face of

Sally Ann Franklin looking at me. Saved.

"Done, you got it, Rhonda." I could hear her smile. "But I gotta go. Someone's calling, gotta get it—call me back as soon as you have it!" I hit the Answer button on the screen.

"Sally, how's things?" The light turned green and I motored past Independence Hall.

"Lance Carter, where have you been? I've been worried sick!" I could feel the worry coming through the phone in her voice. "Are you OK?"

"Sally, Sally, Sally..." I started in a soothing tone, "I'm fine. It's this case. It's been crazy. So much to look into, you know how it is."

"So everything is OK?"

"Yes, everything is fine. In fact, I'm running down a huge lead right now."

"Does it have anything to do with your office being robbed? So dangerous, I hope not. If they were here..."

"No, Sally," I lied. "I'm sure they are unrelated." Sometimes reassuring people is just the right thing to do. Then an idea hit me. "How much access do you have to real estate records?" I knew she had access to everything.

"Me, oh well, everything bought or sold is public record. Everyone can access that information. Why?"

"Can you give me the records on a few addresses? I need to know if someone named Ming ever bought or sold any of these addresses." I gave her Jennifer's old apartment, Lindsey's old apartment, the address of The Moshulu and on a hunch the address at the Packard Building.

"Sure, I... I'll go look it up right now. Give me about an hour?"

"An hour. Call me back." I hung up and stared up at

The Moshulu. A beautiful site to behold with the Benjamin Franklin Bridge in the background. I noticed the charred blacktop in front of the main gangway and the cover that usually extends over the top was missing. Must have gotten burned up last night.

* * *

"What can I get for you, sir?" the short haired young bartender asked. I looked into his brown eyes taking in his black island themed shirt with white flowers all over it. It was quite the look.

"You're awfully stylish, aren't you?" I joked. He stared back at me and smiled.

"Uniform, ya know? Beer?" He prodded. There were about half a dozen people sitting at the bar, some talking, some just watching the flat-panel television hung over the bar.

"How about a lager?" I asked and waited as the bartender filled my glass. The dark wood that appointed the bar ran all the way around and served to accent the wooden beams that ran across the ceiling from one side to the other. The dance floor was lovely, but empty at this time of the day. The bartender returned with my beer.

"Thanks, hey..." He stopped and came back. "Is Roger here today?"

"Yea, of course," he said. "He's here every day."

"Oh, great. Can I talk to him for a minute?" The bartender nodded and disappeared into the lobby area. A minute later, a tall Asian man in a similar black island shirt with a slightly different flower pattern appeared before me at the bar.

"Good afternoon, sir. I'm Roger, the bar manager.

How can I help you? Is everything meeting your expectations?"

I nodded, sipped my beer and reached into my pocket to produce the picture of Jennifer. "You helped my friend." He picked up the picture and I saw a smile run across his face before his eyes darkened.

"No, I don't know her," he said simply, putting the picture down.

"I'm Jenny's friend and I know you are lying." I looked toward the closet door in the back corner of the bar. "You let her stay in that room to help her when she lost her apartment." He looked up and away from me, exhaling at the same time. "She told me. I need to know why."

"Why?" he repeated.

"Yes, why. Why would you help a stripper you don't know? Especially when you know who she was hiding from." I took another sip of my beer and locked my gaze on his eyes. "Why?"

"Look, man," he put his hands on the bar and leaned his weight toward me, "have you seen her? She's smokin' hot. I used to *request* her at the club. Man, I'd get off every time she'd swing those hips on me. Why did I help her? I thought if I helped her… you know…" I put my hand up and looked away from him.

"Yea, you'd thought she'd fuck you, right?" I stood, grabbed his shirt and yanked him hard across the bar. "Or did you assault her? Did you force yourself on her, asshole?"

The fear ran across his face and gripped his features, "No, man, I swear! I never touched her! Well, I mean, I touched her…" a pleasant smile visited his face but I dropped an elbow into his chest, "No, man, you know, at the club!" I dropped him onto the bar. He stood there rubbing his chest.

"That's it?" I looked around seeing everyone in the bar staring at us. The other bartender was backing out of the room toward the lobby.

"I swear, man..." he was still rubbing his chest, "man, that hurt. I could have you arrested. That's assault."

"Do you know Ram Don Ming?" His face changed instantly.

"No, man, fuck you. I'm going to have to ask you to leave. Beer's on the house." Roger turned and walked away. Roger knew Ram Don Ming. Now I knew how Ming knew where Jenny was.

Chapter Sixteen

Smoke on the Water rang out as I walked into the lobby of the Ben. I saw Sally's face smiling back at me. I answered.

"Miss Sally, tell me what you've got."

"It's very odd, Lance. Mr. Ming doesn't actually own any of those addresses now. He did own the one apartment on 12th and Locust but not anymore. All of those addresses, except The Moshulu, are owned by some company."

"The same company?"

"Yuppers," she sang into the phone.

"All of them?" I couldn't believe my ears.

"Well, all except The Moshulu, like I said."

"That company wouldn't happen to be Sparkle Industries... would it?" I asked as I put my hand to my forehead already knowing the answer.

"Well.... yes. How did you know that, Lance?"

"Because that's just the kind of peachy news I was afraid of." I ran my hand up through my hair and stepped out of the lobby back out on to the sidewalk outside the Ben to consider my next move.

"I don't know if this has any bearing on what you are looking for but Mr. Ming had owned the warehouse in the parking lot that is adjacent to The Moshulu for fifteen years, but then eight years ago Sparkle Industries bought it from him."

"What?"

"Do we have a bad connection? Can you hear me? I said that eight years ago..."

"Yea, yes—I mean, I heard you." My tone was reaching exasperation.

"Oh, sorry..." she offered out feebly.

"No, no, Sally. I'm sorry. I didn't mean to bite your head off there... it's just this case. It's all a bit too close to home."

"I am not sure what it is that you are working on exactly but if you ever need anything else please don't hesitate to ask. I'm here for you, Lance." She sounded so genuine and sweet.

"Thanks, Sal. You're the best. Oh," I'd almost forgot, "does Sparkle own the Packard Building address too?"

"Yes, Sparkle Industries owns that but they lease it out. When I ran the check on the Packard building it looks like they own most of that floor and apartments on other floors as well."

"All leased out?"

"All leased out." I nodded my head, affirming what I already knew. "The apartment I gave you, is the current tenant named Sanderson?" Again, knowing the answer.

"No, it is leased to a Lucy Smalls."

"Really?" Clearly wrong, I was surprised but I wasn't sure that it made a difference. "Sally, I think you can do me one more favor."

"Anything you need, Lance."

"Really?" I asked picturing that white blouse again. "Scratch that thought..."

"What?" I didn't answer that.

"Can you get me the apartment numbers and names of the lessee's in the Packard that Sparkle owns?"

"Sure… what does this Sparkle Industries do anyway?"

"Sally, when I tell you that you don't want to know you just have to take my word for it." She did and we hung up. Sparkle Industries owned all those properties. But what was in the warehouse by The Moshulu? As I glided out off the elevator toward my apartment I thought it was time to snoop around that warehouse. I had some leads but no real information.

There were two things I knew for sure; I thought as I opened the door to my apartment. I knew Jennifer and Ram Don Ming were interconnected but I couldn't find the lynchpin that held them together. Was it Lindsey? If so, how and why? Was Ming her dealer back in the day?

"Cowboy!" Linc greeted me.

"'Sup?" I inquired as to his current status, mood and Jennifer too with one, simple word.

"Girl's in your bedroom on the computer. No movement otherwise."

"Roger that, big guy. We need…" There was a knock at the door. I walked over and peeped through the aptly named peephole and saw the lovely features of Nathalie looking at her watch.

"Hey girlfriend," I announced as I swung the door open. "What brings you by my humble abode?" She smiled and produced a take-out bag of Chinese food.

"A little sustenance to keep the big, strong private detectives sharp." She gave me a one armed reach around hug and pushed past me, tossing the bag on the dining room table in the same motion as dropping her purse on the floor.

"I don't eat this food," Linc snarled at the bag.

"What?" Nathalie looked confused. "I got some veggie things, some kung pao, some beef stir fry?" She looked from Linc to me. "No good?"

"No," Linc stated, "no good." He looked at her intently.

"Nathalie, thanks for the food and I'm so glad you're here. Linc and I have to go check out a lead together. Can you hang here? Just keep Jennifer company?"

Nathalie looked crestfallen. "Yea, I guess. You mean I have to eat all this myself?"

"No," I answered digging into the bag and pulling out an egg roll. "I'll eat this one!" I motioned to the door. "Come on Linc, let's roll." Linc lead the way out the door and down the hall. Once in the lobby I explained what Sally had uncovered about Ram Don Ming and the different locations.

"You think he's hiding something in that warehouse?"

"He's owned it for fifteen years. There's got to be something in there. Records of something he's been in to. Maybe something that links Jenny to him or Sparkle in some way."

For the second time today my Camaro rolled into the parking lot adjacent to The Moshulu and I stared at the weather-worn yellow aluminum framed warehouse that has occupied this space ever since I could remember. The building sported a big sign on top that stated in big, red block lettering: PIER 51 STORAGE

"Looks just how I remember it," I said, mostly to myself.

"It looks abandoned," Linc said, looking at the unlit signage. Dusk had fallen and it was clearly dinnertime on The Moshulu. People were milling about on-deck and there were a number of cars parked in the private lot across the street. Linc walked up to the front door that was flanked by a six food wide by three foot tall picture window with the blinds pulled on it. Reaching of the handle, he tugged at it twice confirming that it was locked. Locking back at me, he pulled a club from his belt and put it through the glass in the door with one smooth motion.

"I think the door is open," he remarked as he reached inside the door, unlocked it and pulled it open. Sometimes he can be such a funny guy. I followed him through the door into the musty front office area that looked straight out of 1975. The linoleum floor was probably, at one time, the same color yellow as the outside of the building. Now it just looked like dirty, worn plastic. There was a lime green counter about five feet into the area that secured a wooden swinging door to one side with two grey metal desks behind it. The desks looked like they were abandoned just like the outside of the building. They had nothing on them, not even chairs to keep them company.

"When was the last time you think someone was in here?" I asked looking up at the water-stained drop ceiling tiles.

"I'd say sometime in the last day?" Linc said handing me a snipped zip tie.

"Where'd you find this?" He pointed behind the counter where I saw there were droplets of blood and one golden hoop earring. I knelt down to get a better look at the earring. "Buddy, I think this is a crime scene. That is Linda Sanderson… or Lucy Smalls or whatever her name is—that is her earring."

"The butchered girl?"

"Yea, that one."

"And guess who just got their DNA all over

everything here," he stated. It wasn't a question.

"Shit," I stated matter-of-factly, getting back up to my feet.

"Did we just get set up, cowboy?" Linc asked walking into the back room. I stood and followed him into the back room.

"I think so... maybe we should...get..." I stopped talking when I saw the wall. It was plastered with pictures and press clippings. I took two steps and saw the pictures were of Lindsey and Jennifer. I looked at the candid shots of Jennifer when she as ten, then a little older and then she was a young woman walking down the street.

"Cowboy, I think they've been watching your girl for a very, very long time."

"Yea..." I stammered. "I think you're right." I pointed to the picture of Lindsey. "That's her mom." I reached out to touch it, maybe she'd know I was here. "But why? I still don't know why."

"Cowboy." Linc was standing at the wall staring at a picture. He pulled it down before I could see it, he handed it to me. "Look at this."

I stared in utter disbelief at what I was seeing. It was Carolyn, wearing platform high heels and not much else. She was on stage peering into the camera with a vacant stare that was very reminiscent of a drug-induced haze. I felt my blood boil and my heart race.

"What the hell does Carolyn have to do with this?" I shouted. I started to crumple the picture, but decided to fold it into my pocket instead. "I think we need to send a message, Linc."

"Done." He said as he started pulling the pictures and clippings down one at a time. After about ten minutes we had all the pictures down. Linc disappeared to the car and came back with a can of black spray paint.

"You just carry that around?"

"Yes," he said and began writing on the wall in deft strokes. After he'd finished we stood back and admired his work.

We're on to you.

Simple yet elegant – just one of the many qualities I admired about Linc. We left the building, leaving the front door wide open on the way out. After I'd telephoned my good man Fishkit and reported the "break in", we were back on the road heading to the apartment. No sooner had I hung up with Fishkit's voicemail than my phone buzzed. I answered with a grunt.

"Lancey? That you doll?" It was Rhonda.

"Yea, it's me. I'm having a bit of a day. Find anything?"

"I just emailed over those phone records you asked for. Did your lady friend have a guy in the government or something?"

"I don't think so, why?"

"Lotsa calls to and from DC and Virginia. Same two numbers over and over. They are government numbers. Seemed odd. Check the e-mail, you'll see the address."

"Thanks, Rhonda. I will. I appreciate it."

"What?" Linc grumbled.

"Intrigue, my good man… intrigue and mystery."

"Sounds like a day at the beach," was all Linc said the rest of the ride. The car rumbled into the space in the parking garage. I let it sit for a long moment just rumbling. Linc looked over at me but didn't say anything.

"Is the intrigue that major?" he asked. I didn't

answer right away and he didn't wait for it. "I'm out. Call me if you need me." The door clicked open, slammed shut and he was gone. I savored the sound and feeling of the car for one more minute and killed the engine. No sooner had the enveloping motion of the engine died away that I felt my iPhone buzz in my pocket. I clicked the screen on and saw the text message

> *O'Brien, Gabby*
> *Mt me Wash Sqre pk — 5 min. Revolution. PDQ!*

Now that was something I wasn't expecting. I was exactly five blocks from Washington Square Park. If I ran, I could make it in five minutes.

So I ran.

Chapter Seventeen

The sky was overcast by the time I reached the park. This picturesque respite in the middle of the city was originally designed in 1682 and named Southeast Square. The open-space park served as the southeaster corner of the city of Philadelphia as laid out in William Penn's original city grid that featured five parks in total. One at each corner and one in the center of the city. This park had been transformed several times throughout history to serve the needs of the budding country. Initially just a beautiful respite from the hustle and bustle of busy colonial America and a place for the city's African American community to bury their dead it was then was then transformed into a Potter's Field. When the Revolutionary War engulfed the land it then became a burial place for the dead soldiers. Soon thereafter, Yellow Fever gripped the city and the dead were interred here. But as the fever broke and the city returned to normalcy, the park began to host farmer's markets and camp meetings. In 1825, the park was renamed to Washington Square in honor of George Washington and the efforts made by the soldiers during the Revolutionary War. A monument to Washington was planned but never built. In 1952 the city put a lot of money into renovating and beautifying the park. The City Council decided it would be a more fitting tribute to the soldiers to, instead, build The Tomb of the Unknown Revolutionary War Soldier. And as I stood staring into the fire that was a constant beneath the statue of George Washington, my eyes rose to meet the words inscribed on the tomb:

Freedom is a Light for Which Many Men Have Died in Darkness.

I mouthed the words silently as I read them with my eyes. Any time I came to Washington Square I thought about Tommy. Tommy and I were the oldest of friends. We'd known each other since high school. Went to college together and even joined the Navy together. After the Navy, we didn't see each other as much. He'd had a hard time readjusting to civilian life after Iraq. I kept telling him it was post-traumatic-stress but he kept telling me he was fine through the vodka and rum. He kept telling me that he just needed more time after each sniff of blow. I knew he needed help, I just didn't know how to help him. I remember spending hot summer nights and cool fall evenings sitting beneath the oak by the memorial on the bench. The last time we sat here, it wasn't summer at all. It was the February and it was cold. The steam rose from his breath when he said, *"I'm going to stop Lance. I'm quitting cold turkey."* I was so happy. I was so proud of him I told him we had to celebrate! It was the one week later that February and there was three inches of snow on the ground when they found him. He told me he had an apartment over off Fairmount near the park. They found him huddled in one of the cells at the Eastern State Penitentiary. He'd burrowed his way into one of the closed off sections of the historic prison. He could have frozen to death. He could have died in that hole like so many had before him. I remember getting the call. I remember rushing to Jefferson Hospital. I remember the doctor's balding head, thick black rimmed glasses and tired eyes. They said he had pneumonia. They said they'd found him in time. They said he'd be OK. He died two days later in that hospital bed. That was about a year before Carolyn's death. I was so engrossed in the moment and the inscription that I didn't notice the elf-like person standing next to me.

"Absolutely mind boggling how many people died." Gabby said with reverence. "I mean, revolution is something that is such a part of our culture and yet... we resist it at every turn." She turned her bespectacled face to me and smiled a bright and friendly welcome.

"Gabby?" I asked knowing the answer.

"And finally we meet." I was greeted with the biggest hug from one of the littlest people I'd ever met. She was dressed in khakis, a long sleeve black shirt that minimized her small waist and accentuated her ample bosom. Add to that a black backpack that she carried over one shoulder and the look was compete. Geek-chic! Looking at me, she threaded her arm through mine and lead me to the side of the Tomb, where a bench sat overlooking the monument. She sat and invited me to do the same, crossing her khaki covered legs and pointing a blue flat shoe at me.

"Why did you need to meet with me?" I asked with an edge to my voice. "Why so urgently?"

"What?" She looked hurt. "You didn't want to meet me?"

"No, no.. that's not it. You're the best and..." I made a show of looking her up and down, "you're quite beautiful too. You didn't mention that on the phone." She blushed but didn't acknowledge the comment any further.

"Two things and one of them isn't a phone thing."

She looked around, making sure we were undisturbed and no one could here her. "First, I found your MacBook. It's at this address." She handed me a piece of paper that had the address of the #1 Velvet Dragon warehouse written in a red flowery scrawl.

"Why doesn't that surprise me. These guys have been nothing but a pain…"

"Lance," she interrupted placing her small pale hand on my knee. I looked down admiring the purple nail polish and gold Claddagh ring on her middle finger. "Remember you called me and asked me to look into that file you couldn't access?"

"Lindsey Collins? Yea."

She leaned in and whispered, "That file is classified Lance. As in, government classified." She nodded her head at me as if to head off the inevitable disbelief that I was about to express.

"Were you…" She shook her head and closed her eyes as she pulled away. She pointed to the entrance to the park and stood. I stood with her and began walking toward the entrance. She laughed and smacked my shoulder.

"I am almost certain I am being watched," she said with a giggle. "I don't think they can hear what we are saying but I'm pretty sure that they can hear and are watching. From the time I pulled the information to the time I texted you wasn't long enough for them to get a full blown surveillance team out on me… and you." She looked up at me with another smile, "but it was enough time for them to dispatch a couple of goons to tail me."

"What did you uncover, exactly?" I asked, smiling and playing along.

"Your friend, Lindsey Collins, does not actually exist. Her real name is Laura Palmer and she was in the CIA for almost twenty years before she was killed in the line of duty. Her death is listed as an execution by foreign hostiles and also marked unsolved. The suspect list is short, Lance. And Ram Don Ming is at the top of that list." I couldn't keep the smile on my face.

"Ming is on top of the list? Mother..." She reached up and put her manicured finger to my lips while stopping our walk.

"No, you can't freak out here." She shook her head slowly, her red curls swung back and forth with her head. "I need you to lose the negativity or it might pique someone's interest. We don't want to make anyone any more interested in us then they already might be." I stared down into the green eyes trying to bring something up within them but was failing miserably.

"Lindsey..." I stopped, looking away from her gorgeous eyes. "Laura was my friend Why... I mean how could I not have known this?"

"Deception was her job," she tweaked my nose, "silly!" That made me laugh at myself for just a second. But I still couldn't muster up a smile that stuck.

"I'm trying to wrap my head around everything this could possibly mean. And what it means now for Jenny. Ten years ago, when Lindsey... Laura was murdered people were after Jenny. I got in the middle of it and pulled her out but now people... specifically Ming, are after her again."

"And you're in the middle." she said matter-of-factly and I nodded in response. I looked back into her now clouded emerald eyes. "If you're here, then who is standing between Ming and Jenny?"

"I've got someone with her, she's safe."

"Safe?" She looked at me questioningly.

"Yes, safe. We've been watching her. Ming isn't

going to get to her." She didn't look convinced.

"I've dealt with these types before. They are tough and they treat women like animals. That business that Ming runs, the club, it's just a front."

"I knew it. The dancing and grinding is bad enough. Jenny told me what some of the other girls do."

"Is she mixed up in that?"

"No," I shook my head, "Ming wants her for some other reason. We don't know why."

"I really hate scum like Ming. Human trafficking... abusing women no matter the age is disgusting." I look at her and sensed something else there. Something in her eyes flared and then it was gone. "OK, no more serious talk." She smiled. "How can I make you smile? Have I told you today how undeniably handsome you are?" Her teeth sparkled against the soft lavender shade of lipstick she had on. I smiled back unsure of what to do with that compliment since I hardly knew this very attractive girl in my arms.

"How old are you, Miss O'Brien?"

"I'm twenty-seven and that's Doctor O'Brien to you!" I shook my head in feigned disbelief.

"Too young for me!" I sighed under my breath.

"Too young for what, exactly? Come on," she laughed, poking my stomach. Her faced turned serious and she ran her hand over my midsection. "Nice... firm. Not bad for an *old man*." She laughed pushing me away while continuing to walk, "Isn't it fun pretending to be a couple." We turned and continued our walk out of the park and across the street and down 8th toward the Ben Franklin House.

"Why, not a fan of *couples?*" I asked.

"Hell to the no." she said with no reservations.

"Relationships aren't my thing. Me, my machines and their data. That's my happy place." I nodded as we entered the lobby of The Ben and crossed over toward the elevators.

"Coming up? You could meet Jenny and Nathalie."

"No, thanks. I think this is far enough for the charade." We stopped and looked at each other. "Lance you need to be careful with whatever you are doing. The guys at #1 Velvet broke into your office, stole your MacBook and maybe even killed your friend who was a highly trained CIA operative. These guys aren't amateurs." The memory of being in the back seat of the green Caprice flashed in my mind.

"We've already had a meeting or two. They aren't exactly experts either." I laughed.

Shaking her head at my insolence she added, "Shut up and hug me." She wrapped her arms around me and we embraced for a moment. Just long enough to look familiar not long enough to make us uncomfortable.

"What?" I yelled after her, "No kiss?" Her hand fluttered a goodbye as her feet carried her our the door. I was about to push the elevator button when it dinged softly followed by the doors wooshing open. I took a step back to allow people to get off the elevator.

"Carter," barked Mr. Simpson who lived across the hall from me, "what the hell is going on at your place? You havin' a damned party?"

"What?" I stammered at the older man as he shuffled towards me.

"Damn dog's barkin' his fool head off, people yelling. I have half a mind to report you to the office!" Simpson growled while pushing past me.

"Barking?" There are times I'm eloquent and times I'm not. This is one of those *not* times. So I just go on the elevator and pushed the button. I was still shaking my head when the doors parted at my floor. My heart began to race as the sound of Copper's angry barking shot down the hall. He was angry. It was one of his *this is my territory, you get the hell out* bark. It was very unlike Copper. I'd only heard it once before. When the plumber let himself into the apartment and I was in the bathroom. Copper's not a big dog, but he can make himself sound like a German Shepard. This was Copper, the little Shetland Sheepdog, channeling his inner German Shepard. I slowed my pace and approached the apartment with a cautious deliberation. Shadowing the wall parallel to my door, I couldn't see anything that look amiss. Aside from Copper's ferocious barking and Mr. Simpson's comments, there was nothing to indicate that anything was other than normal. When the door swung I could feel the intensity in Copper's bark coming from the bedroom. I made a move to go to the bedroom but caught movement in my peripheral vision. My body slammed against the wall instantly for cover.

"Mister Carter," the voice bellowed from my living room with a hint of a middle eastern accent that I just couldn't place, "don't be shy. Come on in. Have a seat. It is, after all, your apartment."

Standing there, frozen in my own apartment listening to Copper losing his mind I knew I had to make a decision. So I did.

"Hey," I waved at my guests. There were three of them on the couch. "Holy shit!" I exclaimed. "Buddies!" There, sitting on my couch, were Sleeves and Crucifix. "How the hell have you guys been? I've missed you so." Keep it light and fluffy. "Copper, go lay down boy." I yelled back to the very unhappy little dog. He growled a degree of unhappiness and then was quiet.

"Mister Carter, do you know who I am?" The newest of my friends asked.

"I..." but he wasn't about to let me finish.

"I am Mustafa Soriano."

"Yes, I..." he put a finger up to quiet me.

"Shut the fuck up, Carter." Sleeves and Crucifix stood with menacing looks on each of their faces and showing a piece at their sides. "Do you know who I am?"

"I'm pretty sure you just told me. You're Mustafa from the Lion King. Right?" Soriano gritted his teeth. Kind of looked like he wanted to hurt me.

"Do you know," he began and took a deep breath trying retain his composure, "who Mister M is?"

"Mister...." I put my finger to my chin in thought. "Hey, I've got a question for you there Lion King." Soriano's gaze cut through me. "I left two lovely ladies here and," I made a show of looking around the room, "I don't see either of them here. You wouldn't..." Sleeves took a step towards me. I pulled Betsy out and directed her to him. "You stay over there." I looked towards Crucifix. "You can sit the fuck down."

Simultaneously, Soriano stood and I heard the door to the apartment open behind me taking me off guard. I swung my head around to get a look and saw Nathalie waltz into my apartment looking like she'd just returned from shopping.

"Hey Lancey, surprised?" Before I could react, a blow to my ribs came from one side and as I was doubling over a kick to the gut came from the other. My vision went blurry momentarily and I fell to one knee.

"Now, Mister Carter... or can I call you Lancey?" Soriano laughed. "Miss Tomai, here, has been gracious enough to invite us in. We can't have you pointing your gun at us now can we?" One of the two goons took Betsy from my weakened grip with ease. I looked up and watched Nathalie cross the room to where Soriano stood and lean into him like a cat in heat. The two locked lips and mashed various body parts into one another for what seemed like eternity.

"You fucking bitch," I roared.

"Come on, Lance. You didn't really think you could get this," she waved her hand across her waist, "on your own? Did you?" She paused for a second and gave me a *poor-you* look. "Oh my, you did!" She threw her head back and laughed a cackling laugh that made me want to shove something sharp and rusty down her throat.

"It was you the whole time! Every time I walked out that door you were on the phone telling these cocksuckers where I was going!"

"Wow!" Nathalie feigned shock. "It only took you this long to figure that out!" She smiled her cat-like smile. "You're not a very good detective, you know."

"I trusted you!" I spat out and sprung to my feet only to me be met with a devastating blow from Sleeves knocking me to the floor unable to breath. "Where.." I struggled to catch my breath, "is..."

"Miss Collins? You needn't worry yourself with her for the time being but I do have someone who wants to see you. My friends, whom I think you are well acquainted with, will take you where you need to go." Soriano grabbed Nathalie's ass and pushed her in front of him. She giggled a high-pitched laugh and ran from the room. Soriano was almost out when he turned back. "And they won't fuck it up this time!" A boot to the head made sure I had no say in the matter.

Chapter Eighteen

"Lance, she's in trouble. Where are you?" the voice was urgent and prodding. "You said you'd protect her! You promised me!"

"Lindsey, I know. I promised."

"She's in trouble, she needs you! You broke your promise! This is your fault, Lance Carter!" Lindsey's voice was loud in my mind but I couldn't her anywhere. I could feel tension all around but everything around me was clouded in a dark drab cloak. There were shapes by I couldn't make out anything that I recognized. Nothing that would tell me where I was or what was going on.

"Uncle Lance!" Jennifer's voice screamed.

"Jenny! Where are you? Can you hear me?" I yelled but got no answer. "Lindsey, where is she?"

"Lance, save her…" the voice trailed off as the light became brighter….

* * *

Something warm and wet ran down the back of my neck. Droplets of sweat dripped one by one from the end of my nose. The air was thick with hot moisture making me more uncomfortable then just being tied up would normally be. Not like that is normal or anything. To add insult to injury there were loud humming sounds coming from all around me in this enveloping darkness. I couldn't tell exactly where I was but it certainly wasn't the Hilton.

"Freedom is a light for which many men have died in darkness…" I said out loud and heard only the sounds of the machines around me. "And I am here, in the darkness." Out of that darkness I began to hear the sounds of foot falls. Someone was coming towards me. It came across suddenly, sensed it but not fast enough to do anything. It hit me hard across the side of the head exacerbating my pain and knocking me to the hard, cold ground. My head hit the concrete with a thump hard enough to make my vision go black, then fuzzy and then began to come back into focus. The foot steps were now surrounding me and my own consciousness was tentative at best. I squinted hard to try and focus on the feet walking in circles around me, doing my best to try and count how many people there really were. Was it four? Five maybe? My vision did not improve. "Who…" I coughed, spitting blood. "Who's there?" There was only a laugh in answer to my question. I tried to lift my head but something wasn't right. A bolt of pain shot from my head down my spine. I wasn't going anywhere -- at least not on my own power.

"Mister Lance Carter," his voice bellowed through the bowels of the building as his thickly accented English mangled the words. It sounded Cantonese to me. "I'm so disappointed! I thought you'd put up more of a fight after all the headaches you caused all my men. I was expecting… oh what do you say?" He paused as if he were searching for a word. "Ah, yes… open a can of whooping ass?" He laughed hysterically. "But here you are!" I was wrong, the dialect clearly sounded Mandarin in origin.

"How does the American saying go? Came to shit but only farted?" The laughing continued. "Maybe you should shit or get off the top, Mister Lance Carter!" His hysterical laughter was getting on my nerves but this time he had company. I could detect two other distinct and familiar voices.

"No, boss," a voice interjected laughing, "it be shit or..." he grunted out loud a the same time I heard a thump from the direction of his voice. It sounded a lot like Wade.

"I know, you dumb shit," the voice I now identified as Ram Don Ming said angrily, "you are not correcting me! Turn on the fucking light, you imbecile." A light came on. Foot steps came towards me quickly, then a shuffle. "So, Lance... can I call you Lance?" He paused as if he were waiting for a response. I chose not to offer one. "Alright, Lance it is. So, Lance here we are. I'm standing here above you. You are there lying not the ground like dirt. It is as it always has been. You know that, do you not? You are there lying on the ground like worthless dirt, that is my ground by the way. I own it. You are bleeding to death all over it. What a mess." He chuckled softly to himself. I looked up at him and put my best scowl on, which was not all that impressive at the moment being that I couldn't actually lift my head up.

"I think..." I began to choke out.

"You are bleeding to death, Lance Carter. You may not believe it but this moment and in this place is where you will die. You turned out to be not very tough Mister Lance Carter."

"I think," I coughed out while struggling to open my eyes and focus on him, "that is a vast overstatement you small piece of..." a kick landed squarely between the shoulder blades effectively ending my ability to do anything but moan and cough.

"You, Lance Carter," his repetitive use of my name was really irritating, "are in no position to be talking.. how do you say in English?" He fumbled for words and I could hear him snapping his fingers, "Oh yes, talking the trash out! Is that right Wade?" There was no answer in spite of the incorrect euphemism, "I have to tell you Lance. Your language and its slang it is very challenging at times."

I took a deep breath and coughed blood. "You... seem... to have... a pretty good... grasp... asshole." Breathing became increasing difficult and I fell into a coughing fit.

"Well," he began in a royal tone, "thank you Lance Carter. For that bit of the gratitude I will have Wade and Maurice kill you just a little bit faster."

I regained my composure and was finally able to lift my head and see the blurry Asian-son-of-a-bitch. "Your language skills are strong considering what kind of foreign piece of shit you are. You take innocent and desperate young girls and turn them into your little money-making machines. Their bodies aren't your personal ATMs you piece of..." Since my eyes were wide open now, I saw the black boot coming toward my face. I saw it, but there was nothing I could do about it. It connected with my jaw with a sickening combination of smooth and crunch. Not at all like peanut butter.

"No, Lance. You misunderstand the nature of my business." Ming spat the words at me.

"Business?" Cough. "You're a flesh peddling..." this time it was a fist that hit me hard. Consciousness waned out than back in again.

"I take good girls in. They are good but useless. They have no future and I give them one. This is a life of luxury that they could never imagine. They would not know it but for me. They would not know the silk and the lace. They would not know the lobster and the caviar. So you could say I make the good girls be bad girls. It is true that some of the things they do maybe their father would be ashamed of. These are things maybe they thought they would never do but I give them a life that they could never have. They are richer then they ever imagined." I heard him stand and walk away from me. I focused my eyes and saw Ming standing with his back to me flanked by Wade and Maurice on either side. "But I know what you are thinking. Sometimes they do not listen. Sometimes they will not do as they are told. That must be dealt with swiftly and with an iron fist. It is like any other business." He turned and faced me again. "You can understand that? You are a business man yourself." He looked at me, almost as if he expected my approval.

"You turn young girls into whores who hate themselves. You took Jenny and made her into a self-loathing woman. And there are a hundred just like her." I angrily barked at him. I could feel my adrenaline start to pump. My head began to clear. I struggled to push myself up on my elbows. "You are less than human you dog."

"Jennifer? Yes. She is not your average girl," he rolled the word around his mouth. "She isn't a whore at all, Lance Carter. She has something I need and I will get it from her if I must cut it out of her."

"If you hurt her…" I growled.

Ming crouched down so close to me that I could see the disdain in his flat brown eyes. "You think you can try and stop what I am doing. Your government think that maybe they can lock me up? Throw away the key, as you say?" He laughed. "You can never challenge someone like me, someone as strong as me." He beat his chest with his fist. "You don't have it in you Carter." He looked me up and down. "You are weak, just like every other American. Soft and weak." He stood and backed off. "I'm just as American and honest as you. You sold out your best friend, didn't you? Just to save your girlfriend, right? Who is worse, Lance? Me or you? Me for taking people who want money and giving it to them -- at a personal price, yes. Am I evil for taking people who want the companionship of a pretty young woman and giving that to them -- again at a price. Everything has its price..." He was quiet for a moment and then his voice was lower, more grave in tone. "Am I worse then the man who killed your girlfriend and your best friend because of your lies? Because of your inability to take action? I take action Lance. I know about your precious Carolyn, Lance. I know about Tommy. Do you know how I know?" I stared at him with a new intense hatred. I didn't know how he knew but I knew he was going to tell me. I hadn't thought of Tommy in years and their deaths had nothing to do with one another. Except, of course, me. "Because I was there. I made sure Carolyn got what she needed to end her suffering. I made sure she was dead. But you Lance... you failed. I made sure that Tommy didn't suffer anymore in that hospital bed, what did you do Lance Carter? At least I succeed in what I do. So who is the better man, Lance? Who?" He tore open his shirt to reveal a tattoo of an Asian inspired dragon holding a torn American flag in its mouth. "Yes, Lance I'm red, white and blue and I don't care. I'm just like you. Red, white and blue and tattooed." Next he rolled up his sleeve to reveal another tattoo. This time it was Chinese lettering on his arm with a Chinese flag above it. "I love my country and I love yours. Red, white and blue... I'm your all American nightmare..." he stopped one more time, searching for the right thing to say. Once he had found it he looked at me and slowly spat the words at me, "Mother -- fucker!" Now the smile broadened, "Wade, Maurice... kill this shitbird." He turned and his foot falls were heavy as he walked away down the corridor.

"Where is she!" I demanded. "Where is Jenny??" But Ming didn't stop. "I'm nothing like you!" He didn't turn around. He just disappeared into the darkness. And I was left with Wade and Maurice.

"Hey... guys!" I began with a weak smile. Maurice stepped up, grabbed a fistful of me and yanked me to my feet. My head swam. Maurice dragged me with one hand to the wall and put my arms up into shackles I had not seen before. One clicked closed and then the opening chords of *Smoke on the Water* rang out, echoing down the dark corridor. Wade and Maurice looked at each other in confusion. Apparently in their haste to get me down here, they failed to relieve me of my phone. It continued to sing, so I reached into my pocket and retrieved the phone. Neither of the goons made a move, they continued to look lost. So I answered the call.

"Hello?"

"Lance?" Linc grumbled through the phone. "Where the hell are you?"

"Excellent question." I looked at Maurice. "Hey, Mo. Where am I?"

"Give me that," Maurice stepped up and grabbed my phone. He stood there staring at it for a minute, apparently unsure as to what to do next.

"Get rid of it," Wade rolled his eyes. Maurice looked at the illuminated screen and tossed the phone out of site. It clanked and clacked on the concrete, skidding to a stop.

"Come on..." I yelped. "That's brand new!" I leaned off the wall, pulling at the shackle to test it. It was just a touch loose on my wrist. I thought it I pulled just right I could get loose. "Mo, you owe me a phone!" Maurice answered me with a fist to the gut.

"Shut up!" Maurice screamed in my face.

"Come on man," Wade urged him, "let's get on with it!" Maurice apparently agreed. He pulled a long and dangerous looking dagger from his belt and tossed it from one hand to the other, feeling its weight.

"I'm gonna cut you up like a filet o' fish mothufucka." I glanced at Wade only to see him pull a pistol from the back of his pants.

"I'm sensing this isn't going to go well for me, is it?" I asked hoping to buy enough time to come up with a plan to get out of here. My head hurt and my sides ached, but I still felt pretty confident that if I could get my hand free I would have a fighting chance.

"No, cracker man," Maurice said while walking toward me. He pointed the dagger at me, "now I'm gonna make you a shish-ka-blob."

I held up my loose hand, "Wait. A what?"

"You heard me. A shish-ka-bob." Maurice stopped about three feet from me.

"No man, that's not what you said." I laughed at him.

"He's right." Wade chimed in. "You said blob."

"No I did not. Wade, you shut the hell up. And you," he pointed the dagger at me again, "shut the hell up too or I'm gonna really make this hurt."

"More than a shish-ka-blob?" I inquired hoping to make him stop again. But it didn't work this time. Maurice snarled at me, twirled the dagger in his hand and lunged towards my chest. I parried the best I could with my one hand, pushing the dagger to the side. It caught the side of my shirt but missed my flesh. Unfortunately for me, his elbow did not. It came up and hit me hard on the side of my nose causing it to explode in a bloody mess. Maurice pulled away and turned the blade in his hand again, preparing for another run at me. Suddenly he pulled up short and fell to the ground like dirty laundry. I began pulling at my shackle to get loose, while trying to hold my nose to stem to flow of blood. I glanced over and saw Wade's large frame standing over the limp pile of Maurice looking very confused.

"What the…" and then Wade followed suit landing almost directly on top of the prone Maurice. I stopped what I was doing and looked around frantically.

"Wade? Maurice? You guys dead?" no sooner did the words pass my lips than the formidable form of Linc Diesel toting a short-range sniper rifle appeared out of the shadows.

"They shouldn't have turned on the light." He muttered. "I forgot my night scope. It would have at least made it a challenge. Turning the light on just made them ducks on the pond." He stopped in front of the two lifeless bodies and looked at me.

"Man, am I glad to see you." I told him.

"I know," was all he said in reply. Then behind him came a small, thin figure. Appearing in the light looking particularly sexy was the bronze-haired beauty named Gabby. She picked up her hand and pointed a Taurus 9mm at me.

"Hey now, Gabby!" Without a word she squeezed off a round and the shackle on my left hand exploded. "Ouch!" I yelped shaking my hand. "That hurt like hell!"

"You'll be fine, you big baby." Gabby smiled and laughed at me. Linc tossed my iPhone to me. I looked down and saw the screen was scratched but otherwise the phone seemed to be fully operational.

"You'll probably want a new one. It's all scratched and stuff." He turned and walked back into the shadows.

"Nice shootin' there Texas Tina. Where'd you learn to do that?"

"I did mention I did some work with the government, right?" She smiled sideways at me with a twinkle in her green eyes. "Come on," Gabby waved me along and disappeared with Linc. I followed as quickly as my aching legs would allow.

"So to what do I owe the sudden appearance of The Wonder Twins?" I shouted as I struggled to catch up. Gabby responded by holding up her iPhone, turned and began walking away.

"It's called FindMyiPhone, kinda like FindMyMac but different -- remember?" She shouted back at me, turning and now walking backwards. "You have it on your phone. I can find you anywhere, anytime as long as your phone is on."

"Ah," I said limping along as quickly as I could, "I see.

"When Linc called you it was to see what happened to you. We could tell you were in trouble. I followed the beacon and poof." She raised her hands in a feigned regal gesture. "Here we are! It was that easy. You were just lucky they didn't take your phone from you when they brought you here."

"Yea. Tell me about it. Speaking of... where are we, exactly?" I finally caught up to them as we approached a set of concrete stairs that led to a metal grated platform and a steel door.

"The warehouse in South Philly." Linc answered

beginning to climb the steps and not looking back at me. "We need to leave here."

I began up the steps as fast as I could but I my sides were screaming in pain. "Where is Jennifer?" I asked hoping for an answer other than...

"We don't know..." Gabby said quietly. "But we will find her."

Chapter Nineteen

"Where did the A-Team van come from?" I asked as
Gabby pushed the button to unlock the doors on an all black
full size Chevy van. She pulled the side swinging doors
opened and motioned for me to get in, so I did.

"It's mine." Gabby said simply following me into the
van. "I like to travel in style."

"No kidding…" I remarked looking around. The far
wall of the van had a black leather couch that ran from
behind the driver's seat to the back door. The couch
blocked one half of the back of the van, but the other looked
like a normal door. The other side of the van, where the
swing out doors were, had a small counter with a built in
cabinet above it that looked more like the security panel at
Fort Knox. There was a large, flat piece of black glass that
had several blinking green lights lined up down one side.
Linc found his way into the passenger's seat and swung it
around to face me after I planted myself on the couch.
Gabby's tiny body made its way to the counter. She pressed
a button on the van remote and the side doors closed almost
silently. Then she placed her index finger on a small black
pad on the counter. All of a sudden the glass lit up with
about a dozen different images moving at once.

"Damn…" I muttered in amazement. "What you got

going on in here girl?"

Gabby smiled, not looking back at me. "I'm good at what I do, Mister Carter." She was moving her hand on the counter in a back and forth motion with the occasional poke and prod making things dance on one screen or another. A few taps here, a swipe there -- one screen disappeared, another moved somewhere else on the glass.

"You're telling me." I said.

"This here," she said pointing to what looked like security video footage, "is the security camera for the #1 Velvet warehouse. I'm scanning through it backwards from the time you were brought in." She swiped and tapped again. "This one here," another point to a different location, "is the security footage from your hallway at the Ben Franklin House."

"From where now?" I asked surprised. "How can you..." she put up a finger.

"Shhh." Gabby put a finger up. "I'm good at what I do, remember." She smiled at me and winked towards Linc.

"What else can you do?" I asked, not expecting an answer.

"Being with this one," Linc nodded at Gabby, "reminds me of being in Iraq."

"I'll take that as a compliment," Gabby said swiping and tapping some more. "I have an image recognition routine running on all of these feeds," she motioned to the two she showed me plus two others that I didn't know what they were. "If Jennifer shows up in any of these feeds in the last twenty-four hours, it will alerts us. In the mean time," Gabby leaned forward and reached between my legs.

"Hey..." I jumped back in surprise.

"Lance," she smiled up at me at what I can only describe as a pleasing angle, "it's not that kind of party."

She pulled open a drawer from beneath my seat in the couch and produced what looked like a medical kit straight out of the military. She popped open the large case and pulled out several monitor patches. She plugged them into something below the glass that I couldn't see and then turned back to me holding up the sticky patches.

I smiled. "Where are those going?"

"Take your shirt off please, sir." She smiled back. I did as instructed but winced with each difficult motion. "These will scan your body and give us some data." She began placing the patches on my forehead, shoulder, chest, side and back. "Let's see if you're seriously injured." She said turning back to the glass. She tapped on the glass which brought up what looked like one of those monitors at the hospital. I could see my heart rate, blood pressure and what looked like a slowly forming picture of my upper body.

"Are you a doctor too?" I asked jokingly.

"No, I was a medic in the Marines for two years." She answered deadpan.

"You learn something new everyday." I shook my head.

"When I was alone with Jennifer," Linc began, "I slipped a GPS tracker in her pocket. She should still have it on her. Here is the GPS tracking code." He handed Gabby a slip of paper.

"Nice one, Big Diesel." She slid over looking at the paper. A swipe and a two taps brought up the Philadelphia city grid.

"Four-three-seven point six-two-nine." Gabby spoke clearly as the GPS software registered the tracking code. There was a blinking red dot in the middle of the screen about the size of a backgammon chip.

Philadelphia Story by Bruce A. Sarte

"How long will this take?" I asked.

"It really depends on where she is. It might take a minute, maybe ten." Gabby answered plainly.

"What is all this? I mean I knew you were into tech. That's why I call *you* when I need something. But this?" I said waving my hands around.

"When I was eighteen I was in love." She began. "I met this guy my freshman year at MIT and thought he was just it. The sun rose and set in his eyes and all that romantic bullshit." A whimsical smile traced her pink lips. "Until the first time he hit me. It was stupid, really." She retreated a little into herself. "We were at dinner and he'd ordered a steak and I ordered chicken. The waitress brought out two steaks. I," she paused for affect, "didn't really care. I mean, I'm not a big steak girl but it's not like I'm a vegetarian or anything. I told him it was fine and I would just eat it but he was having none of it. He called the waitress over and was making a big deal when I interrupted and told her it was fine and not to worry. He told me to shut up and backhanded me across the face." She wiped at her nose, maybe at the blood that was no longer there. "I was livid. I got up and stormed out of the restaurant." She looked down and got just a little quieter. "He followed me out to the car. He got in my face, yelling and screaming. I was scared. He hit me. He hit me in the face," she touched her face, "then again in the face. When I fell he kicked me. I cried out but no one helped. He picked me up by my hair and punched me so hard he broke my nose." She ran a finger across her nose. When I looked I could see just the hint of a ridge there. "That was the first time. The next time was at a party and he beat me so bad I spent three days in the hospital." She laughed. "Then I was tired of it. The third time I fought back. I kicked him in the balls and watched him writhe on the floor. But as I started

162

to walk away he grabbed my ankle and I fell hard and hit my head on concrete. It knocked me unconscious just for minute, I think. But when I opened my eyes there he was standing over me. All six-foot-four inches and two hundred thirty pounds of the hate-filled asshole. I was flat on my back staring down the barrel of a gun. I had never been so scared in my life. I thought he was going to kill me. I thought this was it, I am going to die right here on the ground. Lucky for me campus security showed up. He ran like the spineless weasel he was but they caught him." She shook her head. "I promised myself that would never happen again. That I would never be helpless again." She looked straight into my eyes. "All this you see here is my ammunition. Information, training… that's why I joined the Marines. That's why I worked so hard to work for the government and why I'm so committed to what I do. No one will do it to me again -- and I can help save Jennifer too. I've worked hard to become the woman I am today. The bruises on the outside have healed, the bruises on the inside only make me stronger." The system chummed softly and the red dot began to move and get smaller. It zoomed until finally it was about the size of an M&M and stopped at a location.

"Where is it?" I asked anxiously, leaning forward and then falling back into the cushion wincing in pain. Gabby's pony-tail bounced as she swiped making the map zoom in on the location.

"It's… its right here." She said amazed. "Jenny is right here. She's in the #1 Velvet's club."

"No surprise there," I said gritting my teeth. "Let's go get her!" I tried to get up but was pushed back down by a small pale hand.

"You're not done here." Gabby said firmly. She

looked back at the glass and pointed to the red areas. "You've got a muscle tear here and at least one rib fracture... maybe more. I'm no doctor but you aren't in good shape." She pointed to the screen.

"Yea, hurts like hell. So what?" I said more than asked.

"You're going to need this." She slid open a small panel from under the counter, pushed a couple of buttons and a panel popped open next to the glass.

"This place is like a carnival fun house."

Gabby reached in and out came a bottle of pills from which she extracted a small, white, octagonal shaped pill. She handed it to me and looked expectantly. "Well? In it goes."

"What is it?"

"There are things you need to know and things you do not." She said matter-of-factly. "This, you do not need to know. For your personal safety all I can tell you is it is a painkiller. Take it, you'll feel better. In it goes." She nodded. I decided I trusted her enough to put unknown drugs into my system, shrugged and popped the pill. Roughly thirty seconds after the pill slid down my throat the pain in my side was gone. I could still feel my head, but it was only a fraction of the throbbing that had been going on.

"Holy shit!" I exclaimed. "That is phenomenal!"

"Yea, lasts about four hours and if you overdose on it your heart will explode. So let's move, shall we?" Gabby pushed the button causing the doors to swing open. Linc handed Betsy to me from underneath his seat.

"Though you'd want this."

"You'd better believe it. Let's go kick some serious ass!" I practically jumped out of the van.

Chapter Twenty

The sun reflected off the windows at the base of the warehouse. Linc walked right up to the door, pointed his .44 at the handle and fired twice. We weren't going in quietly this time. We were announcing our presence. The door shuttered with the impact. Linc pulled it open and the three of us moved inside. No one was inside. The warehouse itself seemed quiet, almost too quiet. The wind moved some trash around and the door across the floor sat quiet and seemingly innocent. Linc and I knew what was on the other side. I put my hand on the door and stood still.

"Let's go." Gabby prodded me.

"Gabby, you stay here. Linc and I..." She shot me a *you really don't want to finish that sentence* look.

"Have you met me?" She said just before pushing me out of the way and pulling the door open. She was inside before I could even react. Linc and I followed her into the darkness.

"Any chance you have her signal on your phone?" I asked. Gabby just shook her head. We made our way quietly into the bar area. Most of the lights were off and there was no music. The three of us stood there, our guns drawn ready for anything. We stood there for a solid minute before realizing that there was nobody here.

"I think we're alone." Gabby said.

"I thought you said she was here." Linc stated.

"I did, I mean the signal... it came from in here." She replied perplexed.

"No one's here." Linc stated again, as if no one else had noticed.

"They wouldn't just have her out here dancing on stage. The private rooms are back there," I pointed in the direction of the curtains, "and there are offices over there. Let's check the offices first. That's where I'd be." Crossing a dimly lit bar proved to be more difficult than you'd imagine. We kicked chairs, bumped into tables and made all sorts of other clatter getting to the closed door that led to the office area. The door that read OFFICE was a plain wood door set about a foot deep into a wall. There were no windows or other methods to see inside. We were going in blind.

"I'll push you pull," Linc said to me indicating he would open the door and get out of the way while I surveyed what was inside and took appropriate action. Linc pushed, rolled into the room and I pointed Betsy into the dark and empty room.

"Clear." I said.

"Clear." Linc affirmed.

Gabby strolled into the dark room like she was looking for a can of tuna at the supermarket. "Boys, there's no one here." She said flipping on a light to illuminate a small office area with a desk, monitor, printer and a computer. It was clean, no papers or anything on it.

"What about there?" Linc pointed to another door on the wall about ten feet away.

"Let's hit it," I said. "I got the push this time." I popped the handle and rolled into the dark room.

"Clear." Linc said.

"Clear." I affirmed just before Gabby repeated her entrance and flipped on the light switch. This office was much nicer. It had a nice big glass topped desk, picture window, bookcases filled with books. The desk had nothing more than a lamp on the corner. A large aquarium buzzed quietly on the wall to the right and a wet bar sat fully stocked on the left.

"Well, well what do we have here?" Gabby asked looking around. "Is this Ming's office?" She asked.

"No," the Middle Eastern accent came from behind us, "it is mine." I whirled Betsy around to see Soriano Mustafa standing in the doorway. Linc immediately had his gun trained on Soriano but Gabby hadn't reacted to him at all. She was still standing at the bar not doing anything more than looking at him. I couldn't exactly make out if the look on her face was disgust or amazement. Since he was disgusting and there was nothing amazing about him, I imagined it was disgust. Mustafa looked toward her and cracked a crooked smile. "What do we have here?" He said stepping into the room."

"How about you don't move, scumbag." I insisted.

"You're in my office, Carter." Mustafa spat at me, continuing towards Gabby. "Fuck you!"

"In case you didn't notice," I shook Betsy; "we *are* pointing guns at you. And, well, not to be picky but you're alone." I looked at Linc and then Gabby. "We aren't." I pointed at Gabby and Linc for emphasis. "It's the small things I like to keep an eye on, you know?"

Soriano stopped inches from Gabby. She looked up into his dark eyes with disdain. "Back...up." She said simply but clearly, emphasizing the clearly stated threat with a pause in the middle.

"Your guns mean nothing." He said, locked on Gabby's hateful stare.

"Back up." She said again with a little more force.

"And why would that be?" I asked, a little perplexed by his nonchalant attitude toward our firepower.

The smile stayed plastered on his face. "Because I have something you want. You won't shoot me. I'm the only link you have to your precious Jennifer." I snarled. "She has such nice tits and they tasted so good about an hour ago. But this little vixen here," he licked his lips and began to reach for her, "this one would taste so sweet."

I was about to move on him but Gabby beat me to it. Her knee landed square in between his legs just before she growled, "I said back up, asshole!" She punctuated her sentence with a right foot to the face as he arched forward in pain. The kick sent him reeling backwards with blood spraying from his freshly broken nose. Landing squarely on his back the thug curled up into a ball. He was moaning and holding his nose.

"You were saying?" I stood over him, still holding Betsy just not pointing her at him. Gabby came up next to me and kicked Soriano again, this time in the back I think she was just having fun now.

"You red haired bitch!" He screamed from behind his hands. She went to drop her heel into his side but I grabbed her and shook my head.

"So, you know where she is? Spill it dirt bag." I said kneeling down next to him. That's when he started to laugh. Then the laugh grew just a little louder and then he was laughing out loud. Gabby decided to take the situation into her own hands, or feet in this case.

"Hey, asshat, answer the question." She said placing her left foot squarely on his groin and applying just a little pressure. He stopped laughing and the moaning was back.

"So?" I prodded.

"Go to the pleasure rooms." Gabby removed her foot. "You'll see." He started laughing again. "You will see!" Gabby made him yell out in pain again with a well-placed flick of her ankle.

"You go," she said, "I'll keep a foot on this waste." I nodded to Linc and we raced out of the office and across the bar to where the velvet curtains were parted just a touch. You could see an outline of light between them and they swayed softly as if a fan was blowing on them from somewhere unseen. I stopped just short of the opening and took a deep breath.

"Center yourself, Cowboy." Linc said quietly. I stopped and considered what he'd said. That was enough to center myself. It was time. I slowly pushed the curtain back with Betsy at the ready. I looked left and right seeing the hallway with a number of curtained rooms in each direction. I pointed left and went to the right. Linc slinked off down the hall silently. I watched him poke his pistol in one curtain, look in and move on. I did the same. There was nothing in the first room. When I got to the second room I thought I heard movement as I peered in. So pushed the curtain back and entered quietly. The red carpeting led up to the red leather couch in one smooth line. The walls had what appeared to be red and gold fur mixed together. I assume that would serve to muffle the sound. I flashed back to the night I was here and Jennifer was giving me a lap dance. I shook the image of her barely dressed in black from my mind. I stepped to the couch and turned registering each detail of the room from the immaculately clean brass railing on the far wall to the cabinet which held God-knows-what inside of it. I saw Linc pass the curtain in the outer hallway and quickly made my way to follow him. I saw him move from the next room to the next and then turn back to me before I could reach him.

"No one's here. He's lying. Let's kill him." He pushed past me before I could say anything. Apparently Linc is quite fast because he was already entering the office by the time I exited the back rooms. And three seconds later a gunshot went off. I raced across the room only to see Soriano rolling around the floor in agony, holding his left ear.

"I'll make you deaf in your other ear if I don't find out where Jennifer is in ten... nine... eight... seven..." it was at that moment that *Smoke On The Water* began to ring out. Someone was calling *me now!* Linc stopped counting and looked at me. I looked back as the chords continued to ring out. Gabby looked at me.

"Well," she began, "you gonna get that?"

"Answer that phone? Now?" I remarked in disbelief. But I pulled it from my pocket anyway to see my favorite caller... *Unknown.*

"Shit..." I muttered and slid the slider to answer the call. "Hello?"

Jennifer's dreadful scream of tortured pain reflected off a satellite somewhere in the stratosphere and hurdled directly through my phone, into my ear and cut my brain in half.

"Jenny!" I screamed louder than I'd thought.

"Mister Carter!" Ram Don Ming's voice cheerily greeted me. "Somehow, I knew you'd still be alive and kicking. I knew you were better than to die in a basement. I knew it! You just needed a little motivation. Good for you!"

"Ming!" Anger erupting from me and leaping through

the phone at Ram Don Ming.

"Oh, Mister Lance Carter! Why the hostility?" He sounded genuinely confused. Then he started laughing. "OK, OK, here's it the dilly oh. Did I say that right? Am I using the correctly, Mister Lance? No? Well fuck you anyway."

"I am going to reach down your throat and pull your tongue out you..."

"No," he interrupted me, "you are going to sit there like the useless piece of garbage you are Mister Carter. The girl here has something of mine and I will retrieve it from her no matter what. Do you understand that? We have her tied to an electric chair, Mister Carter. Did you know there was an electric chair in Philadelphia? Neither did I until I took a tour of this lovely place. There is only one, though. I did not know there was only one. Yes, anyway, so we strap her in. Now we are going to cut her until she tells us where the information is. If I could fire up Old Sparky, as you American's call it, I would. Make her dance and jiggle. Oh now, wait just a second. I've already seen her do that. Was quite pleasant." Ming laughed an ugly laugh. "Yes it was!"

"Don't you dare draw a single drop of blood from her or I swear..."

"You swear? Tico, cut the girl for fun." Her scream sliced through the airwaves and sent a chill down my spine. I signaled to Linc and Gabby that we had to move. "Now, we going to cut some more." Gabby was through the doorway already. "Tommy would like what we've done with the place. Goodbye Mister Carter. I hope you said goodbye to your girl."

"Ming.... Ming don't you touch her!" The connection was dead. What does Tommy have to do with all this? My mind raced but I just couldn't make the connection to anything.

"You," Linc said to Mustafa who was still writhing in pain on the floor, "my ugly voice is the last thing you'll ever hear." Linc pulled the trigger on the other side of Soriano Mustafa's head effectively making him deaf. Linc stood and left the room without another word.

"Damn…" Gabby let it hang in the air as I walked by her.

"Where are they?" Linc called out, not looking back as he pushed over chairs that impeded his progress. Gabby and I rushed to catch him.

"I don't know… he said Tommy would be proud of what they'd done with the only electric chair in Philadelphia?"

"There's only one place you'd find an electric chair," Gabby offered as we pushed out into the outer warehouse. I kicked at some papers sticking to my feet. "That would be a prison." That made me stop short.

"I know where they are. Run!" I yelled making a run for the van.

Chapter Twenty-One

The van shot off of Packer Avenue and on to the Schuylkill Expressway at eighty miles per hour. We were rifling past Passyunk when Gabby looked at me.

"Why Eastern State?" She asked.

"That's where they found Tommy. Before he died. The state pen. Ming must have some connection there, some reason that he keeps going back there."

"Keeps going back?" Gabby asked.

"The electric chair at Eastern is locked away." Linc began. "If he can get to it, he'd have privacy. No one would ever know he was there. It is in the condemned wing."

"Well, that at least explains that…" I said still no convinced that was all there was to it. "It's about a twenty minute drive."

"Ten." Linc said as he stomped on the accelerator even harder.

"Lance, there was a case that was in Lindsey's file. Project Red Dragon. It is marked as *incomplete*. Here, it might mean something." Gabby pulled a file from a drawer under the glass panel and handed it to me. "I didn't think it was any more important that anything else she was working on until I realized that this was all Asian mafia related." I opened it and scanned the pages. There it all was. Ram Don Ming, Soriano Mustafa, the business fronts, real estate dealings... it was all right there in black and white.

"It says in this file that the CIA was tracking some information or documentation about something called Dragonfire. According to this, Dragonfire was a chemical that when added to water made it toxic. So much so that if someone ingeste a small mixture of water and Dragonfire it would melt you from the inside. It was rumored to be able to liquefy a person's insides without leaving any chemical signature. No tox-screen would ever pick it up."

"Imagine if that got into the water supply." Gabby said plainly.

"This file says that Lindsey had recovered the secret formula. Doesn't say where she got it from but we can guess Ming was involved. She was going to turn it over to Washington but she never did. She died first..." I looked at the date that Lindsey reported acquiring the formula and thought the time period meant something to me but I couldn't place it. "This date is significant... just don't know why."

"Do you think she was ever going to turn it over?"

I shrugged my shoulders, "I don't know. This date is only months before she was murdered. Its..." I stopped and had my a-ha moment, "it is around the time that Jenny had her appendix removed!"

"So?" Gabby asked.

"So? The two of them disappeared; I mean they were gone for a solid week... maybe longer. No one knew where they were. I don't know what exactly." I turned to Linc, "Linc, this is too much of a coincidence. What do we think about coincidence?"

"No such thing." He said without taking his eyes off

the road.

"No such thing." I repeated.

"We're here." The van screeched to stop outside of Jack's Restaurant directly across from what was once the model for reformation in the United States Prison System. It was now nothing more than a tourist attraction. But inside Eastern State Penitentiary Jennifer needed our help. We stood staring at the imposing facade of the main gates of Eastern. The entire structure was a revolutionary design. The entire structure of cell blocks radiated from one central location and then were surrounded by big, thick, stone walls such as the main gate.

"Al Capone... Willie Sutton..." I said slightly awe struck.

"And now we're going to ice Ram Don Ming." Linc said, handing me some ammunition. "Let's move." And we did. We strolled in through the main doors like any other tourist and quickly made our way though the stone floored open courtyard. There were dozens of people milling about and a tour leaving in the far corner.

"Come on, let's latch on..." Gabby suggested. The three of us walked casually to where the tour group was assembled. A balding mad in his mid-forties shouted, "hey when's this train leaving the station?" The teenage tour guide was clearly a bit ruffled.

"This..." she began, smiling a metal smile, "is my first tour." There was a collective groan from the ten or so people gathered. She put both hands up to try and allay the crowd a little bit. The young blonde girl couldn't have been eighteen and as rifling through some papers on an old, grey, metal desk. "I have to just get my walkie talkie and wait for my supervisor to say we are allowed to go in." She reached into a drawer beneath the table and produced the walkie.

"Here it is!" She announced triumphantly.

"OK, toots, let's vamoose. Shall we?" Another younger man prodded her. This didn't help her confidence.

"Excuse me," I raised my hand, "does this tour include the electric chair?"

Her eyes lit up. This was something she could answer and kill a few minutes. "No sir, I'm sorry. The area where the electric chair is located is currently off-limits. That particular area is in need of renovation to make it safe." Another collective groan. "We will pass by it thoough, it is actually one of the first areas we pass."

"And when exactly would we be passing said area, missy?" The older guy asked in a very irritated tone. Her walkie crackled and a voice said something that I didn't understand.

"Now!" She announced and the crowd gave a weak cheer. Walking into the prison was a surreal experience. The young girl was droning on about inmates and exercise and whatnot. It's funny how people can talk but you never hear a word until it pertains to you. It wasn't until she looked at me and said, "That door with the closed sign -- that's the corridor that leads to the electric chair," that I actually heard the words that were coming out of her pretty lips. I nodded to her and mouthed a quiet thank you making sure to catch Linc and Gabby's eyes.

"And through this corridor we can see where the prisoners would have enjoyed their free time…" the young girl's voice trailed off as the crowd slowly shuffled out of site. The red sign with the word CLOSED imprinted in white letters was a grey steel door. Taking a good look at it, it was obviously a newer door and not one of the originals.

"Shame how they destroy original work to secure places." Linc said.

"How do we get in?" Gabby asked, eyeing up the solid looking hole-filler. I reached over and pulled on the handle. To my surprise, the door swung open easily and without any noise.

"I'm going to say we pull on this."

"Good." Linc said and pushed passed us into the dark hallway. I stepped to follow him but Gabby grabbed my hand.

"Do you hear that?" She asked. I stopped and listened but only heard Linc's footsteps getting further away. I shook my head and took a step but then I heard it, too. It was a muffled scream coming from somewhere down this corridor. My steps turned to a run. Gabby was quick to match my pace but Linc lagged behind. I ran from shadow to light back to shadow and then to light as I passed the cells with a tiny window in each. The dirt under my feet from decades of neglect crunched with each footfall. Before long we were at the end of that corridor and stood with a choice to make... left or right.

"Which way do we go?" Gabby asked looking back to see how far behind us Linc was. He was only about half the way towards us. I looked in his eyes and saw that he thought we should go left. I looked down that way and saw that it looked identical to the other direction. Pulling on Gabby's sleeve I started down the hallway to the left. Each step brought us further into darkness. There were no cells this way and consequently no light from the outside. After about twenty feet I began to doubt the decision and I stopped. Staring down the hall into the darkness it seemed lonely and desolate. Gabby came up and stopped beside me.

"What?" She asked, "Why did you stop?"

I turned to answer her when I felt something touch the

back of my neck. I froze for just a second before whirling around to find nothing. Then I saw something out of the corner of my eye scurry down the hallway into the darkness. I think Gabby saw it too because she took one step back.

"What was that?" She asked with a little quiver in her voice. -----

"I don't know." The silence from down the hall was deafening.

"You did…" Gabby began.

"Yes, I did." Confirming that I too saw *it* go that way. I stared into the darkness unsure of our next move. Suddenly there was soft shuffling sound. Then a scratching and a low moan coming from the darkness followed by footsteps that seemed to come from everywhere all at once.

"I think we need to follow him." Linc said as he swept past us, not stopping.

"Son of a bitch!" Gabby yelled jumping at least a foot.

"You saw it too?" I asked but Linc didn't answer, he just kept walking into the darkness. Following Linc, Gabby and I stepped into the darkness unsure of what we would find.

"Is he here?" She asked in a whisper.

"I… don't… know…" In the dark it is difficult to judge space in relation to time. All I can inure is that it was about five minutes down the hallway when I first smelled it. It was a dry, stale smoky odor coming from the direction we were going.

"Do you smell that?" I yelled out to Linc. I couldn't see or hear him but I knew he was up there somewhere.

"Something's burning." He replied and then I heard his foot falls pick up speed. Gabby and I followed suit in spite of not being able to see anything.

Then out of nowhere Linc screamed, "FIRE!" I was able to see a faint glow from what appeared to be around a corner. We turned the corner to see Linc standing in front of wooden door that had a glow coming through the cracks. The smoke was seeping through the cracks and I could hear yelling coming from the room.

"It's fresh. Only been burning a few minutes." Linc surmised.

"You think it's for us?" I asked.

"Don't know but that would mean they know we're here."

"Ming knows we're here." Gabby said matter-of-factly pointing at writing on the door. In what appeared to be blood a message was scrawled across the wood.

Come in and save the girl Carter!

Without a second thought I gave the door a solid kick and it flew off its old and rotting frame. The door fell to the ground and quickly was engulfed by the flames. Smoke billowed out of the open door frame choking us. Coughing, I covered my face and ran into the room not able to see anything. Once in the room I tried to get a look. The room was about twenty feet across and it had a tall ceiling that went to peak in the center where smoke was gathering. I could see bodies moving on the other side of the room but couldn't make out who they were. They stopped, apparently realizing we were in the room. I could see them looking across at me and then the one on the left raised an arm and took a shot. The bullet missed me wildly but my reaction was to fall to the ground anyway. I heard shots coming from the doorway. I rolled away from the shots and behind a wood box. Jenny had to be in here somewhere. The flames were growing hotter and the smoke thickened. Each breath became progressively more difficult. I coughed again. I could hear coughing from the direction of the doorway but I couldn't see Gabby or Linc. I saw only the muzzle flashes. There was a hacking cough coming from the other side of the room. I pulled Betsy from my belt and rolled around the box. I looked, trying to peer through the darkening smoke to find the source of the coughing.

"Lance!" I heard Gabby's voice yelling.

"Here!" I replied, not sure if it helped her. But the more I looked through the smoke a shape seemed to form in the middle of the room. There was a lump that seemed to be moving. It wriggled to and fro just a bit. Sirens began to wail from somewhere outside and there was movement from across the room again. Gunshots rang out and I saw a spike of light from that direction.

"Good bye Mister Carter!" The voice of Ram Don Ming sang out from somewhere in the room. I looked toward the light and saw a hand waving. A shot rang out and the hand stopped moving. Then it went to his chest and Ram Don Ming fell to a knee. Linc had hit him. My eyes searched back toward the entrance to the room and for just a moment the breeze from the door cut through the smoke and Linc's stood there, his face like a cement statue and his .44 Magnum was pointed directly at the outer door. Slowly he lowered his weapon and gave me a look before the smoke wafted across the room again. The fire kicked up all around me as I refocused my attention on the moving lump in the middle of the room. The sudden introduction of the wind had the smoke moving quickly trying to exit the open door and gave me just enough clarity to see that it was Jennifer tied to a chair... the electric chair.

"Jennifer!" I yelled. I tried to move but my limbs

were heavy. No matter how hard I tried, I couldn't seem to catch my breath. Each intake brought little more than fire-born smoke and the coughing began to overtake me. Dropping to the ground again I began to crawl on my stomach toward the chair. "I'm coming!" I coughed out; sure that she couldn't hear me. I looked up and saw a shape... it was hazy, maybe it was smoke. I couldn't tell but whatever the shape was, it was right in front of me. Just like in the outer hall it stopped for just a moment, made a scuffling sound and then darted towards Jennifer. The movement of the being in front of me created a clear path from me to Jennifer. For a moment in time, the air was clean and I could take in a full breath. Partially rejuvenated I pulled myself along and then as quickly as it had been pushed aside the smoke returned. I finally reached Jennifer and grabbed at her foot. I felt her bare skin under my hands and it was unresponsive to my touch. Was I too late? Did that scum Ming kill her? Was it all the smoke? I pulled up on the chair and saw that Ming's minions had stripped her down to nothing more than a t-shirt and her panties. Streaks of blood stained her cotton white shirt giving a deathly tie-dyed effect. I grabbed her head and tried to get a good look at her face. The result was similar, she was bloody and unresponsive. Panic gripped me from within. I was too late. Putting my ear to her chest relief overtook me, she was breathing and I could hear her heart beating. "OK, Jenny. I'm getting you out of here." I began to remove her bindings, noticing the cuts all up and down her arms. They had been torturing her. Between the fire and the cuts it looked like they would stop at nothing to find the Dragonfire. Even as I untied the last of her binding her lack of response alarmed me.

    "Lance!" I heard Gabby's voice call out. The sirens

were louder now. I stood to try and make myself visible to her before ducking back down to finish freeing Jenny from the chair. It took a great deal of effort to hoist Jenny up, but I got her on my shoulder. I tried once and then again but couldn't stand under her weight. A hand came and took one of Jenny's shoulders, helping me carry her out the open door and into the grassy field. Jenny was sprawled out on the grass when the EMT's came over yelling questions at me. Is she breathing? What happened? Is there anyone else inside? I just sat there shaking my head, not really having any answers. I looked at Gabby and then realized the Linc was still inside. I stared at that door for what seemed like an eternity waiting for Linc to appear.

"Yes!" I screamed just as Linc Diesel emerged from the smoke filled doorway with his gleaming .44 Magnum at his side. He took in the scene, looking for something... someone. He knelt down, touched the ground and then walked over to where we were.

"I hit him but he's gone." he said. And I knew exactly what he meant. "I got his goons. They are over there." He looked off in the distance but my eyes didn't follow. She going to be OK?" I stared blankly at the EMTs while they took Jenny's pulse and then put her on a stretcher. Looking at Linc, I shrugged my shoulders. I had no idea.

"Sir, are you family?" the EMT asked. I considered this question and nodded my head in affirmation.

"Yes, I am." I followed him to the ambulance for the ride to the hospital.

Chapter Twenty-Two

The sun cascaded off the vertical blinds creating a lighting effect on the sheets of the hospital bed that made it appear like my legs were sliced hams. My head turned and I realized that I was on monitors and all sorts of other equipment. My hospital room was barren, white and boring... plus no one else was in it. Shouldn't this moment have been like a move? Where I wake up after saving the girl with a topless Hooters waitress waiting to bring me a beer and wings? Unless... unless I didn't save the girl. Emotion welled up inside me. I failed again. Jennifer was dead and Ram Don Ming got the Dragonfire. In the end, Ming was right... he was a doer... a winner. And here I was, a loser who failed at everything that was ever important. A single, solitary, lonely tear rolled down my cheek and fell to the hospital gown. The door opened a crack and a tiny red-topped head with a bouncy pony-tail popped through.

"Lance?" Gabby probed. "Lance! You're awake!" She ran in and threw herself on the bed embracing me. My reaction was partially shock and still some of that sorrow that I'd felt before. Even with all that weighing me down, for some reason having Gabby here made me feel a little bit better.

"Gabs... thank you for coming."

She pulled away and looked at me like I spoke some strange, foreign language she'd never heard before. "What?" Pushing herself off the bed she continued, "you say that like I wouldn't be here." The way the light poured through the blinds made her green eyes pop like fireworks in the night. She cocked her head slightly and her face morphed from happiness to concern. "Lance, what's wrong? You're alright. I mean, your injuries will heal. Doctor said so."

"I can't..." I stammered fighting to control my emotions. I felt like I was losing the battle. "I failed. I failed Jenny. I failed Lindsey. I failed Tommy and Carolyn. I failed everyone..."

"Whoa, whoa there big-boy." She put her hands up to make me stop. "That's a pretty big burden to carry. I don't know Tommy... and I didn't know Carolyn but I know that Jennifer doesn't think you failed her... at all." I didn't notice the subtle use of the word *think*. "I read Lindsey's file. You didn't fail her. The government failed her, the CIA and all of them. They left her to rot and poor Jennifer has had to live with that her entire life and you too!"

"They are all dead, Gabby! They are all dead and I couldn't help them!" I was almost yelling through the tears streaming down my face.

"Dead? Jennifer? She's three rooms down, Lance." Again she looked at me like I had a screw loose.

"What?" I said like I had just been told Copper had puppies.

"What what?" Gabby repeated. "She didn't die, Lance. You saved her life!" My eyes broadened. I could't believe what she'd said.

"She's alive?" I asked quietly and Gabby nodded

with a smile. "Take me to her. Take me now." I swung legs over and was greeted with intense pain shooting through my sides.

"No!" Gabby yelled pushing me back, causing me more pain in my chest and I groaned. "You are seriously hurt. You need to stay here."

"I need to…" she interrupted me.

"Sit back and shut up. I will get Jenny and bring her here. She's in much better shape than you are. You've been unconscious for three days Lance." What? Three days? "How about I get your nurse to talk to you while I see if Jenny is awake."

"Gabby…" I called out to her as she walked away.

"Yes?"

"You know at Eastern, in the hallway? The…"

Gabby looked into my eyes, "yes, I remember. I saw it too. It was there."

"In the room with the chair. There was a moment… a moment that I couldn't get a breath and I couldn't move. The movement, the entity came back. It came back and saved me."

"What do you mean?" She looked at me questioningly.

"It was like a small cyclone. It was just there in front of me and did…" I paused, unsure of my words, "something that made the smoke clear for just a moment. Just enough time for me to catch my breath and carry on to Jenny."

"Really?" She sounded amazed.

"It saved my life and I guess, save Jenny too."

Gabby laughed. "After all this, a ghost saves all our lives. What irony!" Still laughing to herself, Gabby left my hospital room.

About two minutes after Gabby retreated from my

room a tall sandy haired doctor came in. He checked the monitors and began to explain to me the extent of my injuries. I say a listened in awe as he told me I had six broken ribs, two on the left and four on the right side, a serious concussion, a small fracture in my cheek bone and I'd been treated for serious smoke inhalation.

"All in all, the smoke almost killed you. You are a machine. I'm convinced." The doctor laughed leaving my room. I failed to see the humor. I heard mumbling outside my door. I painfully pushed myself up, hoping it was Jenny only to be disappointed by the grim yet determined face of my old friend, Foster Phishkit.

"Carter, it appears you've done it again." He said solemnly.

"Who? Me." I said without a smile.

"Only you could destroy multiple scenes, one of them a national landmark, keep evil secrets out of the hands of evildoers and deliver some bad guys in the process." He said with a wry smile. "Aside from the destroying a landmark, nice job."

"I didn't start the fire. You can't pin that on me."

"Did you do a number on the #1 Velvet Dragon Club?"

"Yep, that was me. Well, I wasn't alone of course. You remember Linc?"

Fishkit winced at the mention of Linc's name. "Yea, how could I forget Mister Personality."

"So what? Did you just come to tell me how much stuff I blew up? Or what?"

"No," he put his hands up in defense, "I wanted to see how you were doing. When I heard you were finally awake I wanted to come in and thank you for delivering these two to us." He handed me two mug shots. "Tito Ortiz and Luis

Obispo."

"Hey, it's Sleeves and Crucifix. My buddies."

"Yes, we apprehended them at the Eastern State Penitentiary after Mister Diesel shot them. The really good news is it took them about ten minutes to flip and become state's evidence against Ram Don Ming. We can put him away for a couple of lifetimes."

"You got him? You have Ming in custody?" I blurted out hopefully.

"No," Phiskit said, "he had already fled the scene by the time we arrived. In Diesel's statement, he claims he shot him so we've got people at every hospital within an hour of here but so far nothing. Perhaps if someone had, say, called us before charging in we could have been there to apprehend him."

I shook my head. "Dammit. I can't believe he got away."

"He might have gotten away, for now. But we've got a wide and active dragnet out on him. He can't hide forever."

"Yea…" I said wistfully.

"We also apprehended Soriano Mustafa who is now completely deaf, thanks to blown near drums from what looks a lot like gun shot trauma. But of course we can't really tell and really don't care. Either way, Mister Mustafa is going to jail courtesy of the testimony of Miss Collins, and the two goons." The door to my room pushed open behind Fishkit and in wheeled Jenny pushed by Gabby.

"Jenny!" I gushed.

"Uncle Lance!" She blurted. "You're awake!"

"And this one," Fishkit said, "provided all the details and hardware that we needed."

Jenny was smiling and besides the bandages on her

face and arms, looked pretty good. "Heck, apparently I was nothing but a mule and didn't know it."

"A mule?" I said with a question in my voice.

"Yes," Gabby began, "when Jennifer's mom acquired the Dragonfire information she saved it on a micro disk. It's similar to the flash drives and memory cards we use in cameras today. Anyway, she had the card sealed in a silicone and had it implanted in Jennifer at some point... I guess to hide it and keep it safe."

"And," Jenny began, "when I was admitted into the hospital something showed up on an X-ray. Since I was unconscious at the time the doctor's thought it was a problem and operated. They pulled it out and were very confused by what it was."

"We didn't even know what it was until Miss O'Brien told us it was a memory card." Fishkit interjected.

"I pulled out an old card reader and once we plugged it in, it was obvious that these were encrypted government secrets. The encryption algorithm is one only used by the CIA. I *started* to break the code..."

"But we stopped her!" Fishkit said pointedly. "And then we turned over the memory card to the proper authorities. Don't need the Feds beating down my door."

"Yes, this guy," Gabby pointed to Fishkit, "is a wet blanket."

I nodded slowly, taking all this in. "The surgery... when your mom said you were in the hospital. I knew it all had something to do with this. Now it makes sense!" I exclaimed.

"I guess so... I always thought it was weird that I had an appendectomy but the doctor's kept telling me I still had an appendix."

"And this all happened while I was here in the

hospital?" I couldn't believe it that the Dragonfire data was right under our noses the whole time. I stared around the room and listened to Fishkit say his goodbyes and promise to visit again in a few days. Jenny looked like she was going to be alright. The doctor's said she'd be able to be discharged in a few days. I told her she could stay with me and Copper as long as she wanted. After Gabby wheeled Jennifer back to her room she came back to say goodbye.

"I'll come back tomorrow." She promised.

"Thanks Gabby, but I know you have things to do. You've been such a help... I mean you saved my bacon. You quite literally pulled me from the fire."

"Aw, shucks." She smiled playfully. "I'm happy to visit you!"

"No really. I mean it, thank you. But you don't owe me anything." The comment seemed to wound her. Her eyes darkened and the smile faltered.

"I..." She looked down at the floor.

"No, I didn't mean... I wasn't trying to be mean. I just..."

"No," She smiled again but this one was just a little less genuine. "I understand. No need for you to get all gushy. Look, I'm going to go. I'll see you." She ducked out of the room before I could say anything else.

Nice going, Lance.

Epilogue

The warmth of the day wasn't lost on me. No matter what happened or where it happened, I still loved spring in Washington Square Park. I threw the tennis ball and watched my furry little friend chase it across the grass that hadn't quite gotten a firm grip on its green yet. Copper skidded to a stop just beyond where the ball landed, retreated and attacked it like only a sheepdog can. Watching my furry companion sprinting back across the park towards me, I couldn't help but reflect just a little bit on Ram Don Ming, Jenny and everything that transpired recently.

"Uncle Lance?" Jenny's voice shook me from my daydream.

"Jenny!" I stood and embraced her. It had been two weeks since I was released from the hospital and while I was still sore and had aches and pains, I was feeling better overall. Jenny had been released a full week before me and was fit as a fiddle. "What are you doing here?" I asked.

"I came to say goodbye," she said looking down at the ground.

"Goodbye?" I think the hurt came through my voice. "I thought… oh never mind what I thought, where are you going?"

"I've decided to start over. Go somewhere that nobondy knows me. Somewhere were I can find out who I really am. I'm not Lindsey…" she stopped and looked off towards the street traffic. "I'm not someone who I don't know. I want to be someone and I want to know who that someone is. You can understand that, can't you?" Her eyes asked me for understanding.

I nodded my head and took her by the shoulders. "Of course I can."

Copper barked twice at our feet startling both of us. I looked down and the tennis ball was at my feet. Jenny bent down and rubbed Copper's head, which he enjoyed quite a bit. She picked up the ball and threw it, Copper shot off to retrieve the bouncing sphere of fun.

"I'll call you." She promised as she turned and walked away. Copper returned with the ball just in time to watch Jennifer disappear from view and into the street. He dropped the ball and looked up at me. I looked back down and watched the ball bounce once, twice and then dribble to a stop and he gave a low whimper.

"I know buddy. There she goes. Out of our lives again. No worries, she'll be alright." Copper barked twice and picked up the ball again. I guess he was good with it. I was going to grab the ball from him again when I noticed a smiling red head watching me from a bench on the other side of the park. She waved a small *hello* wave and crossed her legs.

"Come on boy, let's go say hi to Gabby."

Copper was already on his way before I finished my sentence.

About the Author

Bruce lives in Suburban Philadelphia with his wife and four children. In addition to writing, he enjoys baseball, playing guitar, reading, church, cooking and being a dad.

Bruce grew up at the Jersey Shore and graduated from Admiral Farragut Academy in Pine Beach, NJ where he first fell in love with reading and writing under the guidance of Jeff Cain and Verne Romefelt. From those early influences Bruce was introduced to and fell in love with Shakespeare, Marlow, Henry James and Nathaniel Hawthorne.

Bruce's other works including *Sands of Time, Towering Pines and The Star of Christmas* are available at all major outlets in both print and eBook formats (Kindle, Nook, iBookstore and Smashwords).

Bruce can be reached on his website: http://www.bruceasarte.com , on Facebook, GoodReads or follow him on Twitter @bsarte and be sure to sign up for his free mailing list on bruceasarte.com!

For the best stories from the best authors come by and visit Bucks County Publishing on the web!

Brought to you by:

http://www.buckscountypublishing.com

www.ingramcontent.com/pod-product-compliance
Lightning Source LLC
Chambersburg PA
CBHW031336170626
46807CB00002B/722